GW00758875

The View from Above

The View from Above

RACHEL NOAM

translated by
Rabbi Avrohom Yaakov Finkel

Bristol, Rhein & Englander
Princeton, New Jersey

Published and distributed
in the U.S., Canada and overseas by
C.I.S. Publishers and Distributors
180 Park Avenue, Lakewood, New Jersey 08701
(908) 905-3000 Fax: (908) 367-6666

Distributed in Israel by
C.I.S. International (Israel)
Rechov Mishkalov 18
Har Nof, Jerusalem
Tel: 02-518-935

Distributed in the U.K. and Europe by
C.I.S. International (U.K.)
89 Craven Park Road
London N15 6AH, England
Tel: 81-809-3723

Book and cover design: Deenee Cohen
Typography: Chaya Bleier, Nechamie Miller
Cover illustration: Tova Leff
Calligraphy: Joy Joseph

ISBN 1-56062-178-8 hard cover

PRINTED IN THE UNITED STATES OF AMERICA

Table of Contents

Introduction / 9
The Main House / 15
Ten Commandments / 19
The Guidance Counselor / 23
Graduation Emblem / 27
Summer Job / 33
My Grandmother / 38
The Six-Day War / 45
Volunteers / 48
Searching for the Truth / 53
In the Army / 57
In the Air Force / 63
Disappointment / 67
Volunteer Work / 72
Murder at the Airport / 75
Leaving the Kibbutz / 78
A Trip Abroad / 82

Body and Soul / 88
Return to Reality / 98
Coming Back to Life / 106
Seeing Uzi Again / 110
Migraine Headaches / 114
Searching for Remedies / 121
The Meditation Settlement / 127
Breaking Away / 135
A Shocking Discovery / 138
A New Dawn / 147
En Route Home / 155
Initial Steps / 158
A New Discovery / 165
Encounter in Yerushalayim / 171
A Jewish Shabbat / 177
Meeting the Rebbe / 184
A Farbrengen / 189
Sightseeing in New York / 194
A Closing Word / 201

Introduction

The story you are about to read is true; it happened to me. It is the startling account of the ascent of a soul to the celestial heights and its return to life. I have attempted to convey the overwhelming impact of this spiritual journey, although I do not know whether a supernatural event such as this can be described at all. I doubt that mere words can adequately portray the reality that lies beyond the realm of the physical world, or whether even poetic imagery can evoke the elevated state of consciousness prevailing on "the other side."

Throughout history, there have been thinkers whose curiosity has been challenged by the tantalizing secrets of metaphysics. In their attempts at explaining its phenomena, they succeeded to a degree in perceiving a trace of the absolute, eternal truth. But the exhilarating sensation of a spiritually uplifting experience cannot be measured or quantified by intellectual research and scientific analysis.

I am quite certain that I am not the only person who has had the privilege of having a glimpse of Heaven and returning to this world. No doubt, there are many people who have had similar out-of-body experiences. Nevertheless, I feel that it is my responsibility to publicize the truth as it was revealed to me, in order to make people aware of their inner resources, so that they will open their hearts and minds to learn the truth about the purpose of life.

My story is not imagined or fictitious. All the events related in this book actually took place. The names of the characters and some of the localities have been changed, but public figures appear with their real names. The episodes described in the book occurred over a period of about twenty years, beginning in the middle of the Sixties and extending into the mid-Eighties.

In writing this book, I do not aim to delve into the hidden, esoteric secrets of mysticism. My purpose is rather to relate my search for the meaning of life in this world in light of the experience I have gone through. I have rendered a factual account of the events as they took place, making no attempt at offering a clinical analysis or suggesting rational explanations. My experiences and perceptions led me to make radical changes in my personal life. They were conducive to making me see life and existence in a new light, to view the world from a perspective that differed radically from the principles by which I had been indoctrinated.

I was born on a *kibbutz* of Hashomer Hatzair, the leftist movement that is based on the socialist-communist theory of a classless society with public ownership of all property. The name Hashomer Hatzair means Young Guard, and its ideology of dialectical materialism denies the existence of God and rejects the Torah tradition that has guided the Jewish people since for more than three thousand years ago. Atheistic socialism ridicules the belief in a Creator. It considers material existence and possessions as the only reality. Communist ideology denies the existence of anything that cannot be perceived with the five senses and renounces all belief in spiritual reality.

In that society, people do not take death into account. The subject of death is taboo; it simply is not discussed or even considered. It is as though death does not exist. It is banished from the mind. People assume that after death there is absolute nothingness, that life reverts to empty non-existence. As I grew up, I often wondered how it could be that an individual, whose life had been filled with emotions, dreams, thoughts and actions, could suddenly evaporate and plunge into a black hole of total nothingness. It simply did not make sense to me.

I often stopped to think about my life and asked myself some very basic questions. What have I really done with my life? What have I accomplished? And the worthwhile things that I have done, did I do them because I thought I was doing the right thing, or could it have been peer pressure that motivated me? Was I driven by a lust for pleasure and excitement? In any event, who sets the criteria for good and evil? What, in essence, constitutes a good deed? Does a mortal man have the power and the right to dictate moral and ethical norms? The most frustrating questions were: Who am I, really? Why am I here, and for what purpose was I created? Why are we all here?

These queries led to more problems: Is the human intellect capable of grasping the overwhelming grandeur of Creation? What is the meaning of man's existence in this world if he is a slave to corporeality and subservient to physical matter?

How can I fathom the supernatural, comprehend the absolute truth of a Divine Being? How can one believe in the existence of a Creator without empirical proof? How am I to understand that our slavish devotion to materialism is nothing but a wall separating us from a real existence, from the infinite?

The miracle that happened to me proved to be the turning point in my life. It caused me to change my life and follow the path of the supreme truth. So many people are looking for the truth but it is hiding from them. The quintessential truth which transcends time and space is revealed only to those who seek it with all their heart, all their soul and all their might, *bechol levavecha uvechol nafshecha uvechol me'odecha*. (*Devarim* 6:5)

If mankind would only have a slight inkling of this supreme truth and of Hashem's supervision over the laws of nature, then life on earth would be filled with blissful delight. But at Hashem's behest, His Presence in this world is cloaked in obscurity; it is hidden. The physical world we perceive with our senses is but an outer shell enveloping an unseen core of a spiritual reality. This idea is alluded to in the word *olam*, "world," which is derived from the same root as *helam*, "concealment, obscurity." Thus, it may be said that the world as we know it—*olam*—is the concealment—*helam*—of the reality that is Hashem. He will reveal Himself in His full glory when He returns to Zion with the coming of *Mashiach*.

For two thousand years, Jews have been praying for the *geulah* (redemption), and *be'ezrat Hashem*, we will merit to witness the fulfillment of this prophecy with the coming of *Mashiach*, speedily in our days.

It is my sincere hope that this book will instill hope in the hearts of those who are despondent and ignite in their souls a spark of *simchah*, of pure spiritual joy. The message I hope to convey is that each individual has a specific mission to fulfill during his sojourn on earth. It was for the sake of fulfilling this assignment that he was created. At the same time, we should be aware that Hashem, our Father in Heaven, loves every single one of us with abundant love. I am the living proof of this.

The Main House

*I*n the afternoon, as the sun began its slow decline from its zenith to embrace the azure waters of the sea, I used to enjoy strolling through the main gate of the *kibbutz*, walking down the road toward the wheat field behind the grove of eucalyptus trees. The golden field which covered the top of a small hill was ringed with trees, like a precious topaz in its setting. Along its north side, a tree-lined dirt road led to the irrigated fields of the farm.

I would sit down on a large boulder on top of the hill, listening to the sounds of sunset. The twittering birds would serenade me as I watched little creatures scurrying off in all directions. In the western sky, the immense ruby-red sphere of the sun slowly and majestically sank toward the horizon. Moved by the peace and harmony that enveloped me, I would occasionally write poetry, but generally I would sit in silence, engrossed in the sunset, a marvel that enthralled me each time anew. In my mind, it was like attending the performance of a symphony orchestra, listening to a presentation of the Sunset Serenade.

The colors of the evening sky varied with the changing seasons, the splendor of the setting sun taking on all the diverse hues of the spectrum. Clouds would appear in a variety of fascinating shapes, reflecting the shades and tints of the waning sun. Toward the west, the outline of the small hills emerged as a magnificent backdrop to the treetops that surrounded the field like a natural amphitheater.

Without fail, the focal point of each performance was its soloist, the setting sun, the superstar of the evening.

At the close of the celestial show, I would linger a while, waiting until the colors of the sky faded into the gray of dusk. Only then would I arise to go back to my room in the *kibbutz* dormitory.

The dormitory which housed the teenagers of the *kibbutz*—we called it the main house—was situated on a hill. It was a complex of two-story motel-style structures, with five bedrooms on each floor, all opening into a long hallway. Stairways, communal bathrooms and showers were situated at the end of the hallway. I shared the last room on the ground floor with my best friend Chavah.

Each dormitory building was connected through a corridor to a large schoolroom where all classes were held. Our entire lives revolved around the dormitory, but we had no separate lunch room. We ate all our meals in the communal *kibbutz* dining room.

I sensed that the arrangement of having all children live jointly in the dormitory instead of with their parents was instituted out of economic necessity rather than for ideological reasons. Ostensibly, it was done to relieve the women of the drudgery and the burden of caring for their children. The truth was, that by having their children stashed away in community centers, the women were free to labor in the *kibbutz*. From my own experience, I can attest that this system did not benefit the mothers, and it certainly did nothing to advance the development of the children. I rather think that it stunted their intellectual and emotional growth.

Occasionally, I took along a friend on my nature walks, but mostly I preferred to go by myself. The solitude gave me a chance to do some serious thinking, far removed from the hustle and bustle of the *kibbutz* and the clamor of boisterous children. The time was the Sixties, the age of nonconformity and hippiedom, when frenzied music was sweeping the world, and the Beatles were idolized by the masses of young people. It was a rebellious generation, growing up in an atmosphere of laxity and permissiveness, and I was an impressionable adolescent. I had many troubling questions, but there were no answers.

I was not what you would call an average girl. In any event, in the *kibbutz* I stood apart from the other youngsters. I was tormented by questions that did not trouble my classmates, or so it seemed to me. I thought that this was because my mother had joined the *kibbutz* as a grown-up and only as a last resort. After surviving the holocaust and arriving in Eretz Yisrael alone and penniless, she saw the *kibbutz* as a refuge that offered her security, sustenance and an environment in which to rebuild her shattered life.

After the atrocities of the holocaust, the ravages and starvation, my mother found peace and solace in the *kibbutz* where she remained after marrying my father. However, she never embraced the Hashomer Hatzair communist *Weltanschaung* of the *kibbutz*, and she would often voice her dissent. In my parents' home, I was exposed to beliefs that were not expressed in other homes. To my parents, the decisions of the *kibbutz* were not infallibly right; often they would strongly oppose rulings that were meekly accepted by everyone else.

Before long, I was chosen as youth leader in the Hashomer Hatzair communist youth movement. I felt very proud of the honor and patted myself on the back for having been elected to a leadership position by my comrades, a sure sign that they thought very highly of me.

I worked with youngsters of a neighboring town. I would go there twice a week, together with the other leaders. We would play with the children, take them on hikes, tell them stories and teach them Russian communist songs. After a few months of this, my enthusiasm gradually began to wane. As a matter of fact, I began to have heretical thoughts, doubting whether my work had any benefit at all. The whole thing seemed utterly absurd. Most of the children in my group came from North African immigrant families. These were children of Torah-observant parents who had come to Eretz Yisrael filled with anticipation of the *geulah sheleimah*, the final redemption.

"How perfectly ludicrous," I said to myself, "for me to talk to such children about the glory of Mother Russia, to tell them stories about the Volga River and gentiles named Ivan?"

Little by little, I reached the decision to give up the questionable honor of being a group leader in the movement. I made up my mind to resign.

Ten Commandments

*O*ne of the features of *kibbutz* life was a weekly meeting of study groups devoted to discussions during which the instructor would try to indoctrinate us with the "truth" they wanted us to believe.

One night, some time after I had reached the decision to quit, study group sessions of this kind were arranged on the subject of "The Ten Commandments." The ten commandments to be discussed were ten principles that had been dreamed up by Meir Yaari, the mentor and mastermind of the Hashomer Hatzair movement. These were meant to be guidelines for becoming "the ideal man" according to Yaari's distorted views. I was particularly incensed at his audacity of giving his rules of conduct the title "The Ten Commandments." For Yaari, a man who had nothing but contempt for the Torah, to use these hallowed words was, in my opinion, an act of sheer blasphemy.

What could have prompted him to call these rules "The

Ten Commandments"? I wondered. Was he trying to pass himself off as a Biblical author? And if he did, why was I required to abide by his rules?

What is the truth, anyway? I wanted to know, searching in vain for an answer. Could anyone presume to know the truth? Is my truth the same as Meir Yaari's? It most certainly is not!

Burning questions they were, problems that weighed heavily on my young mind.

His ten rules of senseless drivel were inscribed in black letters on a large wooden board that was prominently displayed in the classroom. This fraudulent doctrine was the ideological foundation of our education.

Anyone wishing to take part in the give-and-take raised his hand, whereupon the instructor gave him the floor, making sure to keep the discussion on target and steer it in the proper direction.

When it was my turn to speak, I was brief and to the point. "In my opinion," I said in a voice quivering with emotion, "the words written on this board will wither, die and pass into oblivion. I don't believe one word of what is written there.

"It says here," I continued, taking a deep breath while pointing at the board, "that a member of Hashomer Hatzair must be truthful. Well, I'm absolutely sure that no one here even understands the meaning of truth. Least of all Meir Yaari, and he certainly isn't going to tell *me* what the truth is."

I raised my voice and looked the instructor straight in the eye. "I have decided to resign as youth leader, and I refuse to accept my initiation badge."

The initiation badge is the sign that tells the world that a youngster has reached adulthood, that he or she is not a child anymore. In the eleventh grade, at the close of an impressive initiation ceremony, every boy and girl in the movement receives such an emblem, which is then worn proudly on the chest. Receiving the initiation badge represents the fulfillment of a youngster's fondest dream. Never before in the history of the *kibbutz* had anyone turned down this coveted symbol.

When I finished speaking, one could hear the audience gasp. People were bewildered, the meeting thrown into turmoil and confusion. Moments later, some of the young folk broke out in nervous giggles.

"You know, she's got a point there," some of them said, nodding in agreement.

Visibly shaken, the instructor tried to restore order.

"Quiet, please," he shouted. "Please listen to me!"

But the noise did not die down. I had stirred up a hornet's nest. I do not remember how the discussion ended. All I know is that I felt relieved, as though a heavy rock had been lifted from my heart. Still, I did not yet leave the movement, but at least I had dared register my disapproval publicly.

When the meeting was over, several young people excitedly came up to me.

"We liked the way you let them have it!" they said, smiling broadly.

"It's about time someone spoke up," one of the girls said, patting me on my back, "and you had the nerve to thumb your nose at their silly code!"

"The words will wither, die and pass into oblivion," they quoted me. "Wow, that has a poetic ring to it. We didn't know you had it in you!"

The excitement, the jokes and the happy chit-chat lasted late into the night. I was the heroine everyone talked about.

I was in a dither, walking on a cloud, too exhilarated to remember everything that was said.

Things began to change. I realized that I was different and that I doubted the validity of the course the adults were setting for us. It dawned on me that my thoughts were going to put me at odds with the movement line. I tried to be outgoing and sociable. I was going to need as many friends as I could get. It would not be easy, going against the establishment.

The Guidance Counselor

O ccasionally, the *kibbutz* guidance counselor would call me in to have a talk with
me about the importance of the movement and the principles
on which the *kibbutz* was founded. I did my best to avoid him.
I had the impression that he was not up to discussing the
subject in depth and that he was treating me as though I was
suffering from some emotional disorder or social maladjustment. One day, he told me that he wanted to see me in the
teachers' room. This time I could not get out of it, and we
arranged to meet in the early afternoon. When I showed up,
he greeted me with a benign smile, in an obvious effort to be
nice to me and gain my confidence.

"I know that something is bothering you a great deal," he
said, leaning back in his wooden armchair. "I'd like to help you
by talking about your problem. That way you'll be able to
understand why you are behaving the way you do."

Well, I thought, this certainly sounds quite interesting.

Let's hear what he has to say.

"Look, Rachel," he began in a serious tone of voice, "I know for a fact that you are embarrassed by your father. As a matter of fact, I know that you are downright ashamed of him. On the other hand, you think that your mother is a very wise and well educated woman.

"Now let me set you straight, Rachel," he continued, with that trust-me-I-know-better look in his eyes. "You are making a big mistake. Your father is an upright and decent man. He is a nice chap, and everyone in the *kibbutz* likes him. He is a hard-working fellow. The *kibbutzniks* admire him because he is an honest, dependable farmer who knows what he's doing."

The more the counselor talked, the more I realized how far off the mark he was, and that he did not have the slightest inkling of what was really upsetting me. I was close to tears.

Where did he get the notion, I thought to myself, that he could read my innermost thoughts and feelings? Imagine, me being ashamed of my father! Did I ever say I was ashamed of my father? I only wish every Jewish girl had a father as wonderful as mine.

On and on he rattled, and I just tuned out. I did not think it was fair for him to use his authority as a psychologist to turn me into a mental case, just because I had the courage to say aloud the things others kept to themselves.

When he ended his discourse, he looked at me with a smug expression on his face. He was convinced that he had scored a bull's-eye, that his analysis had been correct. According to his evaluation, I admired my mother and was ashamed of my father. As a result—so he thought—whenever my mother would express an opinion that was at odds with the prevailing *kibbutz* philosophy, I would swallow it, hook, line and sinker. It was quite true that I was strongly influenced by the strength of my parents' convictions, but it was a positive kind of influence. They taught me to think for myself, and this propelled me to search for the truth.

The tears welling up in my eyes seemed to reinforce his determination to break me down, but he accomplished exactly the opposite of what he was trying to achieve. I refused to talk. He pressured me to say something, anything at all. But I kept insisting that I had nothing to say.

I knew that it was no use speaking frankly and confiding in him. Since I was not going to agree with his point of view, he would diagnose me as a mental case. Taking advantage of his position, his age and his experience, he gave me *mussar*.

"Either you agree to think and speak properly," he said, "or I'll see that you are marked for life."

"Excuse me," I said, and without waiting for his reaction, I got up from my chair and went to my room.

Releasing all my pent-up emotions, I threw myself on my bed and cried. I realized I was facing a battle with the odds stacked against me. It would be me against the entire *kibbutz*. The pressure would be enormous. Anything could happen. I might be classified as retarded, feebleminded, psychoneurotic or as a case of severe social maladjustment. Nevertheless, I was determined not to give up.

"Never," I whispered to myself, "never again will I speak to this guidance counselor. I've had enough of his guidance. He won't be *my* advisor any more, that's for sure."

My roommate Chavah entered. She was my closest friend, the one with whom I shared my innermost thoughts. I had many other friends, but Chavah was special.

Seeing me sprawled on my bed, bleary-eyed and with disheveled hair, Chavah was taken aback.

"What happened?" she exclaimed. "Please tell me what's

bothering you. Maybe I can help."

"Not now," I replied, managing to smile through my tears. "Some other time, when I've sorted things out. Then I'll tell you everything."

Chavah and I got along fabulously. I enjoyed my heart-to-heart talks with her. We could sit for hours thrashing out a variety of topics ranging from politics to music, anything that came to mind. Sometimes, she would agree with my criticism of the movement, but she loved the *kibbutz* and firmly believed in the Hashomer Hatzair outlook on life. She would talk a great deal about her love of Eretz Yisrael.

"I'll never leave Eretz Yisrael," she would say emphatically. "I love my homeland; I simply could not live anywhere else."

Her words had a hollow ring. She did not sound as though she were expressing her own thoughts. Rather, it seemed to me that she was parroting her instructors and counselors.

Graduation Emblem

A few weeks later—it was the end of winter—the weather warmed up considerably, so that one could go out wearing just a thin blouse. Initiation time, the ceremony when the emblems would be handed out, was rapidly approaching. Excitement filled the air; everyone was involved in the preparations for the big event. A huge raft had been built on the pond behind the dam on the east side of the *kibbutz* to accommodate the graduates. Around the pond, metal posts and posters had been erected, festooned with torches made of kerosene-soaked burlap rags.

The pageantry was spectacular. The entire *kibbutz* population, young and old alike, showed up. I was standing among the spectators, watching silently. My classmates, standing on the raft in the center of the pond, opened the program with a rousing song.

"Silence!" the sonorous voice of the Party leader finally rang out. "We shall now present the initiation emblems!"

The ceremony was reaching its climax. The Party leader called out the names of the graduates, and one by one the students, dressed in their blue and white Party uniforms, stepped forward to receive their badges.

How foolish! I thought. Why are they so anxious to get that silly badge? After all, it's only a piece of metal. And who needs this outrageous, pompous rite of passage?

Still, I was torn with mixed emotions. On the one hand, I loathed the whole asinine exercise, yet on the other hand, I felt as if something was choking me.

"I wish I could be there on that platform, along with all my classmates," an inner voice cried out.

I loved my friends and hated to be left out, but I knew I was different.

I must not give up now, I said to myself. The whole thing just doesn't make sense. This ceremony represents the emptiness of communism; it is all based on lies.

The torches were lit to the thunderous applause of the audience. Suddenly, the entire night sky was illuminated by the huge flaming torches on top of the metal posts, and the audience intoned the *Song of the Partisans*, the anthem of the movement. I felt like running away to escape from the incongruous scene of Jews in Eretz Yisrael celebrating by singing Russian songs. But I was too proud to beat a retreat. I stayed. I felt the people staring at me, wondering why I was not on the float.

The ceremony came to a close, the torches were extinguished, darkness settled again over the *kibbutz*, and the people dispersed and went home. I was walking with my parents, and we were joined by Eliezer Yardeni and his wife. Suddenly, Eliezer turned to me.

"How come you are here?" he asked with wide-eyed

surprise. "Aren't you supposed to be on the raft together with your classmates? Hey, and why aren't you wearing your blue blouse and white scarf?"

"I decided not to accept the initiation badge," I replied impassively.

I did my best to show an outward calm, but in my heart a storm was raging. Clenching my fists, trying to control my emotions, I was on the verge of having second thoughts about my decision. Why did I have to be different? Couldn't I have put up a false front and pretended, just like all the others?

Eliezer was the only one who noticed that I had not received the graduation badge. I detected a look of admiration in his eyes.

"You've got spunk," he said with an approving smile.

He was in his late twenties, ten years older than me. He was married and had a little daughter, but I sensed that he was plagued by the same problems that occupied my thoughts.

A few weeks later, another Party gathering was scheduled. I told Chavah that I planned to make a dramatic announcement in front of everybody.

"I'm going to declare publicly," I said excitedly, "that I'm quitting the Hashomer Hatzair movement. And right in the middle of the gathering I'm going to walk out in protest."

"Sounds exciting," Chavah replied.

"You know something," she said with a glint in her eyes, "I think I'm going to join you. What have I got to lose? The initiation badge I already have; they can't take that away from me."

We submitted our plan to a number of other friends.

"We will demonstrate by staging a walk-out," I explained. "Then we'll march to my parents' house where we'll have a glass of wine and wish each other *lechayim*, as a sign that we don't belong to the movement any longer." (According to the tenth "commandment" of Meir Yaari, a Party member was not permitted to drink wine or any other alcoholic beverage.)

We could hardly wait for the meeting to get under way. We wore our white blouses which were considered festive clothing in the *kibbutz*. The group leader opened the assembly, not noticing anything unusual. We were cracking jokes, but that would normally happen at all rallies.

I rose and asked for the floor. All eyes turned in my direction.

"What I'd like to say is, I don't believe in what we are doing here," I said, my voice cracking with agitation. "I feel they are trying to brainwash me to think along lines that don't seem to be truthful and rational. Until today, I have not yet discovered my true identity, who I really am, but I am sure that some day I will find out."

The words flowed in a torrent. I sensed that I had the audience on my side, and with rising confidence, I continued.

"I don't believe in the ideology of the movement. I don't believe in the Marxist ideal of a classless society, and in my estimation, the so-called "ten commandments" of Meir Yaari are nothing but a pack of nonsense."

I paused to let the words sink in. Then, taking a deep breath, I continued, carefully choosing my words.

"That's why I think it would be hypocritical on my part to remain in the movement. And so, I have decided to give up my membership, and as a token of protest, I am now going to drink a glass of wine and wish you all *lechayim*. Anyone interested is cordially invited to join me."

I got up and left the room without waiting to see what was going to happen. I did not want anyone to try and persuade me to change my mind. As I was leaving, I heard the sound of chairs moving, and to my great delight, I was joined by Chavah, Esther, Chedvah, Tziviah and Irit. Laughing boisterously, we quickly exited and made our way to my parents' house.

We entered the house radiating exuberance, bubbling over with good cheer. I told my parents that we had decided to resign from the Party and that we wanted to drink a *lechayim* to celebrate the occasion. My parents looked at each other with raised eyebrows, as if they did not quite know what to make of the situation, but they readily offered us some wine and candy. We sat for a while, chatting, taking sips of wine and exclaiming, "*Lechayim, lechayim!*" I sensed a buoyant feeling, a fever of excitement, a feeling of relief from a burden that had been weighing heavily on my consciousness.

From now on, I reflected, no one can compel me any more to do things I don't believe in.

Things were looking up, and suddenly, I foresaw a bright future. The time we were made to spend studying the status of the Russian worker, and the hours wasted on discussions in which they tried to convince us of the superiority of a planned economy, all that time we could now devote to studying important things, things that really interested us.

Most of all, I was thrilled that I was not alone, that there were other young people who felt the same way I did.

We left my parents' house in tumultuously high spirits and returned to the main house. The place was in a turmoil. The news of our walk-out had spread like wildfire, and people from other classes clustered around us, bombarding us with questions. We were the center of attraction that evening. To be sure, not everyone agreed with us. There were some who angrily accused us of undermining the organization, of being anti-social and anti-Hashomer Hatzair, whereas others openly expressed their admiration of our actions. The group leader had already left. I could imagine how he must be feeling, and I really felt sorry for him. I felt that our demonstration had hurt him deeply, but I had no alternative. I simply could not continue to conform to the falsehoods of the Party.

The excitement and the discussions lasted until late into the night, but I left quite early and went to sleep. I knew that the action we had taken was only the beginning, that the main battle—the struggle against the adults, the group leader, the Party and the *kibbutz*—still lay ahead of us.

It did not take long before I was labeled an oddball, a misfit and a nonconformist. Perhaps I really was. I did not have the patience to wait for social progress to bring about changes in the life of the *kibbutz*. I wanted immediate answers to the questions that were tormenting me. There was no authority I could ask; I could find no adult who was qualified to provide suitable answers. And there were so many things I wanted to know.

Why, I wondered, was I born here in this *kibbutz* of all places? Why was I born a girl and not a boy? What is death? Why do I dislike *kibbutz* life so intensely?

Summer Job

I did not like the work I was assigned to do in the *kibbutz*. From the age of twelve we were put to work for two hours each day; during vacation time, we worked extra hours. Generally, the work was quite heavy, such as pulling weeds in the irrigated fields. After a full day of studying in school, we would go out into the field, and for about two hours, we stooped over the long rows of cotton or beets, pulling by hand the growth that sprouted rapidly around the tender seedlings. After work, coming back to the main house, perspired and covered with dust, my hands a grayish green, I ached all over my body. My muscles and back were sore, and sometimes, I had a stabbing headache from the sun that beat down mercilessly.

After taking a shower that provided relief of sorts, I would flop into bed, dead tired. The evenings were spent doing homework, and occasionally, there were get-togethers and *kibbutz* functions.

Another job at which I became quite adept was washing dishes. After lunch, I would stand in the kitchen wearing my work clothes, doing the dishes for the five hundred *kibbutz* members. Sometimes I would scrub pots and clean the silverware. After two hours of this, my hands would be white and wrinkled, my clothes and shoes soaked. Nevertheless, I still preferred doing this kind of work to pulling weeds in the fields. Here, at least, I was protected from the blazing sun, and my muscles did not hurt. While washing dishes, I could give my thoughts free rein, thinking about anything that came to mind, and no one would bother me.

A short time after my session with the guidance counselor, I decided that I wanted to get to know my father better. I felt that I did not know him well enough. Although I visited my parents every day, for all intents and purposes, I lived in the main house, and before that, I had lived in the communal children's home. The visits with my parents were relatively short, half an hour to one hour each day, but visiting with parents is no substitute for family life where your character is molded by the familiar principles of ethics and morality. Besides, under the *kibbutz* system, parents did not want to waste the precious visiting hour on instilling ethical teachings that would be of no benefit anyway. They preferred to spend the hour with their children in a pleasant atmosphere, avoiding anything that might lead to confrontation. The fact of the matter was that our parents had no influence on us whatsoever; our upbringing was completely in the hands of the official "educators" of the *kibbutz*. To show respect to parents was not one of the values we were taught in the *kibbutz* education we received, and if we ever did learn of the existence of this concept, it was too little and too late.

My father worked in the poultry house. The only way I

could spend more time with him was by working together with him on the job. To that end, I spoke to the labor administrator, asking him to assign me to work in the poultry farm. He was delighted to grant my request since there were not too many volunteers for this kind of work.

The next day, I began working in the hen house, and just a few days later, I talked the foreman into appointing me as my father's helper. The poultry farm was comprised of several separate large hen houses for egg and meat production. My father was in charge of one of the egg houses, and for two hours each day, he was assigned a helper. It so happened that it was precisely those two hours that I was on work duty. I was extremely happy about the way things were falling into place, and for about two years I worked alongside my father. I would gather up the eggs, clean the water troughs and distribute the chicken feed.

The better I got to know my father, the more I came to admire him. He never admonished or reproached me and never raised his voice to me. He solved any problem that arose between us by gently explaining to me the reasons for his point of view. He was a man of infinite patience, and I do not remember him ever striking me. He had a highly developed sense of humor which he injected into melodramatic theatrics. With the hilarious stories he told he often had me in stitches. I felt that he had a clear grasp of a problem and that I could freely reveal my thoughts to him. Working with him was a wonderful experience, notwithstanding that the work itself was backbreaking and very dirty. Being near my father more than compensated for the discomfort the job entailed. Both of us thoroughly enjoyed the hours we spent together.

I felt sorry for my father, a man of obvious intelligence, who certainly could have advanced to a more interesting occupation, and, instead, had to do such menial labor. He belonged to the generation of *chalutzim*, pioneers, who sacrificed themselves, surrendering their ego, and went about building with their bare hands their dream of the Jewish *yishuv*. It was a generation that gave up the pursuit of an education and spiritual growth, waived normal family life and renounced the comforts of life. Sad to say, in retrospect it is evident that they could have realized their vision without abandoning the Jewish heritage they received from their forefathers.

My father had pragmatic answers to my weighty questions. His explanations centered on the present, on the practical aspects of life. He had a clear understanding of the causes and effects of the developments in *kibbutz* life, but he could not answer my big questions.

"I'll be frank with you," he said. "I don't have the foggiest notion why you were born a girl and not a boy."

And when I asked him about the nature of death, he shrugged his shoulders.

"I must admit, Rachel dear, I have no conception of what death is," he said with a quizzical look. "That's the way nature operates. There's no explanation for it."

I did learn one very important thing from him, a lesson that was to stand me in good stead throughout my life. He taught me to accept whatever life brings even if I don't exactly understand the why and wherefore. Being an inquisitive, vivacious and headstrong girl, I also learned that it is sometimes better not to ask too many questions. It took years, but I learned.

Working in the hen house, I developed an attachment to the birds I was taking care of. I had a distinct feeling that they possessed a degree of integrity all their own, something akin to a soul. As time went by, I developed a strong aversion to meat. Whenever I would enter the dining room to find chicken being served for lunch I would be sick to my stomach. This might be the bird that I fed yesterday, I thought, the bird that looked at me with its doleful eyes. By what right do I eat it? I took the attitude that eating poultry was wrongful and barbaric. Are we permitted to slaughter a chicken, I reasoned, just because the bird is not capable of defending itself? It seemed like an appalling act of cruelty to me.

My Grandmother

$\mathcal{I}$ had a very close relationship with my grandmother, a frail and ailing woman, who lived in our *kibbutz*. In her later years, I would go to visit her every day to sit and talk with her. It was a habit that was ingrained in me by my mother who was very conscientious about visiting Grandmother. Repeatedly, she impressed on my mind the need to respect elders, in particular to Grandmother. My father's parents had perished in the holocaust, and my grandfather on my mother's side passed away a few years earlier, so that Grandmother was my only grandparent.

Whenever I entered Grandmother's house, I would find her engrossed in a book, her glasses perched awkwardly on her nose, her head bent forward, oblivious to the world around her. She was an exceptionally bright person, a woman of uncommon insight and wisdom about life, and whoever knew her loved her. I never heard her utter a harsh or unkind word about anyone. She always had a smile on her face and would give encouragement to all who needed it.

The elderly people lived in a separate section of the *kibbutz*, a situation that acutely annoyed my mother. It upset her to find that the housing of the parents was inferior to that of their children, the younger members of the *kibbutz*.

More than once she voiced her displeasure. "Whoever designed this housing development," she would complain bitterly, "will have to answer for it in a Higher Court." But there was nothing she could do about it.

Every day, I would drop in at Grandmother's house to find out how she was feeling, to talk with her and to enjoy her sharp wit, her wisdom and her profound understanding of life and human nature. She gave me a great deal of practical advice, something my friends in the *kibbutz* never obtained. Her wise counsel guided me during the crucial moments of my life, and through her I made the right decisions. In her final years, Grandmother suffered from a variety of illnesses that caused her much pain, but the one thing that most distressed her was her loneliness and the feeling that she was a burden to the community and to her family.

I noticed that most of her time was taken up by studying *Tanach*. Whenever I came to visit, the *Tanach* was usually open in front of her. One day I asked her why, of all the books, she read only the *Tanach*. She replied by telling me a long story about her early years.

"My dear child," she began, speaking with a far-away look in her eyes, "I was born into a family whose ancestors were driven out of Spain more than five hundred years ago. Generation after generation, they wandered from country to country in Europe, fleeing from persecution and pillage, hoping to find a safe haven.

"I myself was born in Bulgaria," she continued, gently

placing my hand into hers, "but my father who was a rabbi was elected to serve in the rabbinate of a Romanian *kehillah*, so our family moved there while I was still a small child. My father, the rabbi, who taught Torah to the boys of the *kehillah*, decided that I, his oldest daughter, should study Torah along with the boys. He enrolled me in his Torah class and found me a separate seat on the side. So you see, I spent my early years studying Torah.

"When I was fourteen years old, my father suddenly died. My mother and I, her oldest daughter, were faced with having to provide for my twelve brothers and sisters, and so I had to go to work. When I came of age, I was married to your grandfather, who was born in Germany but whose parents hailed from Poland. Raising a family did not leave me any time for studying. But now that I have all the time in the world, I have gone back to my first love: learning Torah.

"Does that answer your question, dear?" she asked, caressing my cheek.

Grandmother lived in a very modest home. It consisted of a small room, a kitchenette and a tight shower cabinet. The front door opened into a small hall, and that was it. It was, in fact, one room in a row of assembly-line housing for the elderly parents of the *kibbutz* population. Virtually all of them were survivors of the holocaust, escapees from the horrors of Nazi Germany who arrived in Eretz Yisrael with nothing more than the shirts on their backs. Now, these people were broken and old, haunted by the memories of their families who were annihilated and their possessions that were taken from them.

Behind the house, there was a large forest, and often, after my visit with Grandmother, I would take a walk through the woods. I needed a walk like this especially after finding

Grandmother wracked with pain, when she would welcome me with weeping and bemoan her bitter lot that she had been doomed to continue living after Grandfather's death.

Often, she would say something that sounded strange to me.

"I only wish I could finally leave the *Olam Hazeh*, this earthly world," she would sigh.

One time, noticing the bewildered look in my eyes, she explained.

"When a person dies," she said with deep emotion, "he does not just vanish into nothingness. He only takes leave of his body; he departs from this world, the *Olam Hazeh*, but his soul passes on into a place we cannot see. This place is *Gan Eden*. That's where I will meet Grandfather, *alav hashalom*, and remain with him forever."

Parting with Grandfather had been very difficult for her, but her belief in an afterlife gave her courage and peace of mind. I did not dare ask her where she had obtained the knowledge of this "other world." I was satisfied, as long as it brought her calm and contentment. The truth is that she convinced me that this indeed represented the best solution for her.

The conversations with Grandmother during the final months of her life turned out to be a guidepost for me regarding the major question that had been on my mind, the question about the nature of death. I understood the underlying message she conveyed with perfect clarity. I sensed her yearning and how she was preparing herself spiritually to leave this world. She gave her explanations in a calm and deliberate tone, with complete acceptance and a sincere feeling that she had completed her assignment in this world. She had fulfilled all that was asked of her.

I was in awe of her, especially in moments such as these. I wondered whether I, too, would be fortunate enough to experience a feeling like this in my life. Would I live up to that which was expected of me? What really was expected of me? And who was making any demands on me anyway? Where did I fit into the scheme of things? I was happy that Grandmother felt the way she did and that she did not have the perception that her life had been wasted. At the same time, I was overcome with sadness. I knew that her days were numbered and that the end was rapidly approaching.

One day—it was about two weeks before her death—I came to visit her. I heard strange sounds coming from her house. Rushing inside, I found her lying in bed, pale as a ghost, gasping for air. She had difficulty speaking, but she managed to utter a few words.

"Don't call your mother," she pleaded in a barely audible voice. "Don't call the doctor. I want to die."

"I promise," I said.

I was stunned. I stood there, looking at her in wide-eyed confusion. This was to be the last time I would see Grandmother alive. I left in a hurry, tears streaming from my eyes. Could I just leave her to die? How could I do a thing like that? But she clearly said that this was what she wanted! What was I to do? To whom should I turn? Luckily, just as I left the house, a neighbor who had heard the noises also came out.

"What happened?" she exclaimed.

I told her.

"Go and get your mother," she screamed. "Run! Hurry up!"

At this instant, I decided I was not going to let Grandmother die. I rushed to my parents' house to call for help. By the time my mother arrived, the crisis had passed. I felt relieved. Feeling that I could not face up to Grandmother's death, I went outside into the forest to calm down. The serenity of the forest, the towering trees and the rustling wind soothed the turbulence raging within me. After that day I could not visit Grandmother anymore. I had pangs of guilt about it, but I simply could not bear watching her languish, barely clinging to life.

Two weeks later, Grandmother passed away during the night, and the next afternoon, the *levayah* took place. My mother felt that I was too young to attend the *levayah* and asked me to stay home. I was not upset. I was happy for Grandmother's sake that her wish had finally been fulfilled. I did not even cry. I sensed that she was now together with Grandfather in that other world about which she had talked to me.

Shortly before the *levayah*, my friend Chedvah's father came to the main house.

"Do you know that your grandmother has died?" he asked.

"Yes, of course," I replied.

"How come you're not sad?" he asked.

"I'm happy for her," I answered naively. "This is what she wanted for herself."

He looked at me with open-mouthed astonishment; he could not believe what he had heard. Without saying a word, he turned around and left.

I must have frightened him, I thought. He simply cannot understand that Grandmother is now in the place where she wanted to be.

After the *levayah*, the family sat *shivah* in my parents' house. I stayed away as much as I could; I could not stand the weeping. The women looked at old pictures, crying all the while and speaking Romanian, which I did not understand. I ventured to ask one of them a question.

"Tell me, please, why are you crying so much?" I inquired. "You are aware that Grandmother wanted to die. She was suffering so much pain these last few months."

"You don't understand," came the answer. "You, a girl raised in a *kibbutz*, couldn't possibly understand what a real mother is, a mother who soothed your woes and dried your tears, to whom you could always turn, with whom you could discuss all your troubles."

With that she again broke into heart-rending sobs.

Noting that my presence was not very helpful, I excused myself and left. Once again, I passed Grandmother's house and realized that I would never see her again. I was sad, but I did not cry. I knew that this was what she had wished, and there was nothing more I could do for her. I went for a walk through the fields.

The Six-Day War

*I*t was the beginning of summer, and the days were becoming warmer. Since I had left the Party, I had more spare time for the things I enjoyed. I became closer to Chavah and Esther, especially to Chavah, with whom I could talk for hours on end. She was a bright girl with a charming and outgoing personality. We would often go for long walks and discuss subjects ranging from girlish small-talk to significant problems that went to the roots of our lives.

One evening we were taking a walk, when suddenly we noticed long beams of glaring searchlights to the southwest sweeping back and forth, piercing the dark night. The sky was alive with crisscrossing flares and flashes illuminating the blackness of the night. Alarmed at the eerie sight, I began to tremble in my shoes. I was terrified.

"Chavah, I'm scared," I said, grabbing her hand. "I have a feeling that something is happening. I don't know what it is, but I'm scared stiff."

I was shaking all over my body, biting my lips to hold back my tears.

"I think you're right," Chavah replied. "I also feel that something's going on. Do you suppose it is war?"

"Yes, maybe it's war," I said with a shudder. "I have a strange intuition, like a sixth sense, telling me that something big is about to happen, something we cannot control, something that is decided by a power we don't know. What do you think it is, Chavah?"

The answer was not long in coming. A few days later, we learned that the armies of the Arab nations were moving forward toward our borders, encircling our country and threatening to wipe out the Jewish *yishuv*. We were terrified. Where could we run? What could we do? There were so few of us and so many of them. Would we, like our relatives in Europe, perish in another holocaust? We were petrified.

The people of the *kibbutz* had no time for talk or speculation. There was work to be done. In the square of the *kibbutz*, preparations were in progress at a feverish pitch. We all joined in, filling sandbags, erecting fortifications around sensitive positions in the *kibbutz*, digging trenches, cleaning shelters, taking part in training exercises to prepare for shelling, bombing raids or enemy penetration. We listened to stories about past wars, about the strategies that had been employed then to drive away the enemy. Life in the *kibbutz* became very confused, tension showing on everyone's face. Old squabbles were forgotten, and everyone pulled together, standing shoulder to shoulder, toiling for the common cause. Work on the fortifications was so exhausting that at night we dropped off into a deep sleep, free of any worries.

Then it happened. On the 6th of June, 1967, war broke out—the Six Day War. We could hear the frightening blasts of the explosions and the din of the battles raging near the frontier. During the night, the skies were lit up brightly by the fire of the distant battlefield.

I could not help thinking that young boys, merely two years older than myself, were fighting like full-fledged soldiers.

How do they feel being caught up in the heat of battle? I wondered. The thought made me feel very small.

This was to be my second encounter with death, but death was wearing a different face. This time, death appeared in the youthful guise of young men fallen in battle, who met their end while in their prime, boys in the bloom of youth who did not have time to live. Why did it happen? Who ordained all this?

The stunning victory in the war brought relief; the fear ended, but the weeping began. The hundreds of young men who had been killed in the war were buried daily in an agonizing outpouring of grief. Death was wearing the uniform of robust young men who had offered their life so that others might live.

I had a guilty conscience.

Do I deserve that anyone should give up his life for my sake? I asked myself. What should I do to be worthy of such sacrifice? How can I prove to myself that my life has a purpose, that it is not one big waste? Where did these men who gave their lives go? What obligation does their sacrifice place on my shoulders?

Their remains were resting in the dust, and my questions were left unanswered, dangling in mid-air.

Volunteers

Summer was at its peak when vacation started. We had one more school year ahead of us before we would be drafted into the Army. Rumor had it that this summer a group of students from the United States was going to arrive to spend their vacation in the *kibbutz* and help with the farm work. The students would be "adopted" by host families who would take care of them during their stay. They would sleep in bungalows, two to a room. In the morning, they would work in the fields, helping out with the farm work or in the dining room, and in the afternoon, they would visit with their host family. I asked the man in charge of the arrangements to place a nice girl with us, and he agreed.

Her name was Judy, the daughter of a well-to-do Jewish family from Cincinnati. She was a lovely girl, slender, with black hair and large dark brown eyes. Initially, I found it difficult to get through to her, but after a short while, I began to talk to her in the broken English I had learned in school.

Our conversation was very superficial. She told me about life in America, and I related some trivial inside stories about life in the *kibbutz*. But I sensed that she had depth. I tried to talk to her about more profound things, about the questions that were baffling me, but she kept her distance, withdrawing into her own shell. It was as though we were speaking on different wave lengths. My English simply was not good enough to carry on a conversation on the level I wanted to communicate with her.

One day, something happened that utterly changed her attitude. I was walking toward the communal dining room with Judy and Chedvah, when Judy suddenly interrupted our conversation.

"The other day," she said, "I was listening to the instructor giving a talk about the movement, about the doctrines of Hashomer Hatzair. Tell me, what do you think of those principles?"

I could tell that she was confused, that something was puzzling her.

Chedvah began to talk about the movement in glowing terms, explaining the many youth activities the *kibbutz* offered and the beliefs on which the movement was founded, about ideological collectivism, equality among all members, Marxism, socialism and more such propaganda claptrap. Chedvah sounded as though she were going around in circles, like talking out of a fog. She did not make sense. When she finished, Judy turned to me.

"Well, Rachel," she said, "what's your idea?"

At first, I tried to evade the issue. Then I decided to be candid with her.

"To tell you the truth, I don't believe in the ideology of the movement," I said. "As a matter of fact, I have quit Hashomer

Hatzair, because I don't agree with their doctrines."

Judy's eyes widened as she gave me a curious look, but she did not pursue the conversation.

That night, I walked her to her bungalow. It was a glorious summer night. The sky was studded with stars, and a cooling breeze brought welcome relief from the intense heat of the day. As we sat down on a bench under a gnarled old olive tree, she asked me questions about the Six Day War. I sensed that she trusted me and had more on her mind than talking about war stories and battle statistics.

"Rachel, why do you think we won the war?" she suddenly blurted out.

"It was a miracle," I replied without hesitation. "A *nes*, pure and simple. There is no rational explanation for it. There's no other way for me to understand how a handful of Jewish refugees, survivors of the holocaust, could deal a crushing defeat to a combination of huge and well-equipped mechanized armies. To my mind, there is no logical explanation for all these mighty Arab armies being smashed by a bunch of Jewish boys and, to top it off, in only six days."

"So you think it was a miracle," Judy said pensively. "But people in the *kibbutz* tell me differently. They think the victory was achieved due to the heroism, the superior skill and planning of the Israeli Army."

"In my opinion," I shot back, "it is ridiculous to say that. I think that our victory is one of the things that cannot be explained rationally. It is quite true that our boys fought like lions, and their self-sacrifice is truly awe-inspiring. It is also true that the fighting was vicious and ruthless. But I don't have the slightest doubt that it was not their bravery that brought about the overwhelming victory. The cause of our triumph is a mystery, the same mystery as that of life and death."

Judy just sat there, lost in thought, staring silently into space. After a brief pause she resumed the conversation.

"You know, Rachel, you are the only person in the entire *kibbutz* who thinks this way," she said. "No one else has offered me this explanation."

"Maybe so," I answered laconically. "I know that I'm different."

It was late. I said good night and went to sleep in the main house. I knew we had broken the ice.

From that day on, we became close friends. How curious, I thought, two girls from totally different backgrounds and yet with so much in common. Both of us enjoyed the outdoors. Together, we would sit and watch the spectacular sunset without saying a word, or we would lie in the grass and gaze at the starlit sky.

"This is what we should offer as the main attractions of this *kibbutz*," I said. "Verdant pastures, glorious sunsets, brilliant stars—and hard work." Entranced by the beauty of nature, I got carried away. "When you think about it, the *kibbutz* represents the ultimate test of the Jewish people's willingness to settle Eretz Yisrael. It is a very tough test, a test many people have failed. But Eretz Yisrael is our land. I don't really know why it is ours; anyway, that's what they taught us in school, that the land is ours, period. Who knows? Some day, perhaps, I will find out the true reason why we call Eretz Yisrael our land and the legal basis for our claim to it. I have changed my mind about a lot of things."

Judy did not answer. She had grown up in America, pampered and sheltered, living in luxury. She had never thought about problems of this nature. We sat together on the grass under the silent, starlit sky, enjoying each other's company without needing to speak.

When I met Judy the following day, she seemed per-
turbed.

"You look upset," I said. "What's bothering you?"

"Hm, nothing, nothing at all," she replied. "It's just that in
a few days vacation is over, and I've got to go home to the
United States."

Only then did I realize how close we had become to each
other.

"I wish you could stay," I said.

"I'd like nothing better," Judy replied.

"Why not?" I asked.

"I have one more year to finish school," she said.

We both felt the sadness of imminent separation. When it
was time for us to part, we agreed not to say good-bye, hoping
that somehow, soon, we would see each other again. In the
meantime, we would keep in touch by writing. As she boarded
the bus to the airport, she gave me one lingering last look,
smiling with sadness. She waved good-bye.

Searching for the Truth

*T*he day of *Rosh Hashanah* went by, and *Yom Kippur* was approaching. I decided to fast in honor of Grandmother's memory. I remembered how the old folks used to fast on *Yom Kippur*. The evening before *Yom Kippur*, they would come to the communal dining room where they would be served a meal, and the next day they would be served a separate meal after nightfall.

We were not taught anything about the significance of *Yom Kippur*, fasting or abstaining from work, and our usual three regular meals were served in the dining room. I did not understand why and for what purpose the older people were fasting, but I sensed that by fasting I would be offering a token of remembrance to Grandmother.

Several weeks passed. One morning, as I entered the classroom, I noticed that Esther had been crying. With tear-moistened eyes, she told me about the terrible accident that had happened aboard the *Dakar*, the submarine that had been lost at sea. Her brother had been a member of the crew. I sympathized with Esther, my heart bled for her, but I had no way of helping her. I felt completely powerless to do anything, as if I were paralyzed.

Once again, death was rearing its head. The reports coming in from the *Dakar* were distressing. The submarine had disappeared, and all contact had been lost. Apparently, it had gone down. I joined Esther in her attempts to find out what had happened to the *Dakar*. We travelled to her parents to be with them during the terrible tragedy. The fate of the *Dakar* was a complete mystery. The submarine had vanished without a trace; no one could say where and how.

Two weeks later, we suddenly heard on the news that the lost submarine had been sighted off the coast near Haifa. Bursting out singing we went over to Esther's parents' house where we found a joyous gathering in progress. Relatives, friends and neighbors were congratulating each other and wishing each other *lechayim*. The house was packed with well-wishers, talking jubilantly about the happy outcome. Only Esther's mother, sitting alone on the couch, staring with a look of resignation, did not seem to share the general euphoria.

"Let's listen to the news," she said in a flat voice.

Someone turned on the radio to hear the newscaster announce that the reported sighting of the submarine had been erroneous. The submarine that had been seen in Haifa was a different vessel. A stunned silence fell over the room. The whiskey cups were placed back on the table. The radio was turned off, and a stifled whimper broke the silence.

Everyone sensed that the submarine was gone forever.

All through that year, our thoughts were with the *Dakar*. Esther refused to concede that the submarine was lost, and her parents, who did not give up hope either, were torn between feelings of hope and despair. The mysterious dance of death only served to heighten the intensity of the questions that were gnawing at me without letup.

Once, on my daily visit with my parents, I was talking to my mother. Out of the blue, she brought up an unusual topic.

"I am aware," she said, "that in school they teach you that God does not exist. But let me assure you, Rachel, God *does* exist. There is a Divine Being, and you should not believe them when they tell you otherwise."

"Why are you telling me these things now?" I asked her.

"Simply because I want you to know that there is a God."

"But Mother," I protested, "in school they told us that this is not true. They told us that you are behind the times if you believe in God, that religion means escape from reality."

I was spouting the atheist propaganda that had been drilled into me over the years, although deep down I knew I was not sure it was right.

"Rachel dear," Mother continued, "my mother told me that there is a God, and my mother never lied. I am telling you on her behalf: There is a God. That's it. Period."

I remembered Grandmother. I recalled her yearning to die, but I could not associate this with what my mother had just told me. Not wanting to get into an argument, I kept quiet.

That evening I went out once again to gaze at the sunset. Sitting alone on my boulder in the field, watching the setting sun, tears welled up in my eyes.

"God, if You truly exist, I want to see You," I whispered tearfully. "If it is true that You are there, why are You hiding? What am I to do if I can't even see You? If I don't see You, how can I be sure that You really exist?"

I was tired. With the sun sinking slowly behind the horizon, my turbulent mood calmed down. The sky was glowing with an enchanting vermillion red tint on an expanse of small billowing white clouds. The solitary rays of the sun cast a shimmering radiance on the majestic scene. The serene tranquility and the beauty of the resplendent sunset filled me with a sense of indescribable joy. Who had created all this? Who is the Master that painted the beautiful sky? Who makes the birds soar gracefully through the sky? Is this beauty the work of God? Is He the One Who made it all happen? Was He answering my question and revealing Himself to me?

When darkness fell, I returned to the main house. I suddenly felt at peace with myself. I knew that everything would turn out all right. Perhaps Grandmother was watching over me from Above.

In the Army

The sweetness of springtime filled the air; flowers were budding, birds were singing, and the heady fragrance of orange blossoms added zest to life.

Judy and I kept up our correspondence. Judy resumed her college studies. She kept me informed about the latest American musical hits, and I played Sergeant Pepper, from the Beatles album she had left me, until I knew all the songs. Thanks to our correspondence and the American records, I passed my English finals with flying colors.

The people of the *kibbutz* were upset to hear me play what they called "decadent American music." To their mind, songs with a fast beat ran counter to Soviet-style music and contaminated the listener's outlook on life. One of my classmates, a dedicated Party member, decided to take action; she tried to grab my broken-down old record player and wanted to run off with it. I had worked very hard to acquire this record player, and I was in no mood to let her get away with it. Like a tiger,

I pounced on her and snatched it away from her.

"This is mine, you hear?" I screamed, my face flushed with anger. "Don't you dare take it away from me. And that goes for all of you!"

She tried to wrestle me, but I let her have it, yelling at the top of my voice. At the sound of the disturbance, my friends came out of their rooms and pulled us apart. From that day on, everyone knew they had better not try to touch my property. They realized I was not to be trifled with.

In the wake of the incident, our counselor found it necessary to give a talk on the subject of modern music. In a profound psychological analysis he explained to us the evils inherent in rhythmic musical syncopation. He explained that the type of music I was playing inspired people to rebel against the Party and its doctrines, that its seductive beat stimulated irresponsibility and looseness. His thoughtful discourse left me cold. I knew that the only reason I liked American music was that it was given to me by Judy.

The school year was coming to a close. I wanted to graduate high school, but for ideological reasons, they did not prepare us in the *kibbutz* for the final exams. As a result, I had plenty of spare time, time to worry about having to join the Army. I was also wondering about Judy; it had been quite a while since I had received a letter from her.

One day, as I was walking down one of the alleys of the *kibbutz*, I bumped into my friend Chavah.

"Guess who arrived this morning," she said with a knowing smile. "Judy has come back."

Together, we hurried over to the main house to find her sitting in the grass under the bougainvillea shrubs in front of the entrance. I was truly happy to see her again.

"Welcome back, Judy," I said, greeting her with a fond embrace. "We really missed you."

"Well, I made it back," Judy said. Her nonchalant tone of voice concealed the deep emotion reflected in her eyes.

We went into my room and talked.

"I had a hard time convincing my parents to let me go," Judy said, "but in the end, they gave in. So here I am."

Judy easily adjusted to life in the *kibbutz*. She joined an intensive course to learn Hebrew, and in the afternoon, she worked in the irrigated fields. Everyone liked her for her sparkling, sunny personality and her diligence. She worked as if she were trying to make up for lost time.

I helped her with her Hebrew lessons, and at night we would relax listening to the records she had brought with her from America. Now and then, Chavah, Judy and I would go to my field on top of the hill to watch the sunset. The three of us would sit there silently, awestruck by the spectacular beauty unfolding before our eyes.

"I have been told," Judy whispered dreamily, "that inside of everything in existence there resides a spark of spirituality. Even plants have such a spark. Yes, you can find it even in water or in an inanimate rock."

It sounded weird, but I knew that Judy was right, that there was something sublime hidden inside Creation. We never spoke about such things in the *kibbutz*. The people there denied the existence of anything other than materialism. They did not believe in a soul or in a person's spiritual needs. They expressed their kind of "spirituality" in songs about nature, in Russian love songs or in studying Marxist ideology. Not a word about the pure spirituality that exists beyond the realm of the physical.

As my induction into the Army approached, I became

more and more despondent. To me, being in the Army felt like a tragedy. I dreaded the prospect of being separated from my best friends and being thrust into a totally different environment.

When induction day arrived, I got up early, packed my things and, together with Chavah and Judy, hitched a ride to the bus station. As I said good-bye to my friends, it seemed as though a chapter in my life was coming to a close and I was embarking on a journey toward an unknown future. I was placing my fate under the control of an unknown authority. I was putting myself into the hands of the Army. For the next two years, the Army could order me around and do with me as they pleased.

It was late in the afternoon when I arrived at the induction center. Most of the girls in my outfit had arrived earlier and were already wearing their new uniforms. I was rushed through the registration process, and after about an hour of filling out questionnaires and giving blood samples, I joined the others on the bus to the training camp. I was not the only one late in arriving. Sigal and Orit, two girls from other *kibbutzim*, arrived at the same time I did, and as it turned out, we had a great deal in common. Then and there, the three of us became close friends.

The next morning, we had our first marching drill. Before long, we were issued rifles and began to practice target shooting. As fate would have it, of the thousands of girls who were inducted in my draft call, I was the only one to be issued a rifle that had a swastika etched into it.

When I discovered the mark of shame, I broke out crying. How could I shoot with this rifle? This might be the rifle that killed my grandmother. How could they do a thing like this to me! The girls, staring at the loathsome sign in wide-eyed disbelief, were visibly shaken by the discovery.

I began to wonder about the source of the weapons we were using, about principles of human ethics, about our right to exist, and all my old questions about life and death surfaced again. But my most perplexing question was this: How did it happen that out of thousands of girls, I was the only one to receive a rifle marred with this blood-stained mark of Cain? Twenty years later, I learned that whatever happens is decided from Above by dint of *hashgachah pratis*, Hashem's close supervision of each person according to his own deeds. But at that time, I did not yet know this.

The next day, we began our training in the combat use of the weapons. When the instructress began to explain the operation of the various weapons, I lodged a protest.

"I'm sorry, ma'am," I said, standing smartly at attention, "but I cannot use my rifle."

"What seems to be the problem?" the instructress asked.

"Ma'am, my rifle has a swastika carved into it," I replied. She registered utter surprise.

"They evidently forgot to erase it," she said.

"It can't be erased," I shot back. "And I refuse to shoot with this rifle, ma'am."

The instructress was quite young and obviously a sensitive and cultured person. Although she tried to present a tough exterior, she could not hide her true refined character. I felt badly for placing her in a predicament, but I had no choice. She did not continue the dialogue, and the next day, she saw to it that I was issued another rifle.

My presence in the Army did not make me feel proud at all. Some of the girls were delighted to be in the Army; they were flushed with pride over their new status and their smart uniform.

I remember a girl by the name of Zoharah who went to the trouble of meticulously rolling up her hair every night. When they would wake us up for marching drill at three in the morning she was heartbroken. She would run around and do the marching exercises with her rollers in her hair. A fastidious girl, Zoharah cared a great deal about her appearance, and every night without fail, she neatly put up her hair in rollers. She was constantly fussing with her hair, as incongruous as this might seem in the middle of training, and her uniform was always spotless.

At the completion of basic training I refused to take part in the swearing-in ceremony. It reminded me of the inane ritual where the initiation badges were handed out. I thought that this, too, was a pointless exercise.

In the Air Force

After basic training, I was lucky enough to be assigned to the Air Force. I had to take an interesting course in one of the most sensitive and important phases of this branch of the service. After graduating the course with high honors, I was dispatched to serve at an air base in the Sinai Peninsula. It was the period of the undeclared war of attrition when bombs and shells fell across the Suez Canal on a daily basis and air battles were fought with sickening regularity.

I tried to do my assignment in the best possible way, but I was different because I did not really like the Army. At the same time, I had enough sense to distinguish between dreams and harsh reality, between what you have and what you hope for. I was doing an important job defending the security and integrity of the air space over Israel. I could not bear the thought that anyone, God forbid, should be hurt because of my negligence. I worked very hard, and my labor bore results.

Coming back to my room in the women's barracks in the evening, bone-tired after putting in a full day's work, I would lie down on my bed and fall into a deep sleep, oblivious to all the perils surrounding me.

I was the only woman in the Air Force sector where I was working. The enlisted men treated me with respect; perhaps they saw me as a mother in whom they could confide. They used to discuss their troubles with me as though I had the wisdom to solve their problems.

The commanding officers, who were career men in the regular Army, were more mature. These were professionals, engineers or experts in their respective fields. All were highly pleased with the way our unit was handling its responsibilities, since within a few short months we had managed to iron out a host of snags and had become a smooth-running operation.

Gradually, I developed a closer relationship with my roommates. We were living together for about a year and a half. During that period, many problems cropped up, such as how to go about obtaining separate meals for women, since it was unpleasant for us girls to eat in the dining room on the base swarming with men. The meals were served at set hours. Hundreds of perspiring young men, like untamed horses, would push their way toward the tables to wolf down immense quantities of food. The ear-splitting noise and the pungent smells that went with the meals hardly need to be described. We, a handful of women soldiers, were the object of grinning leers and snide remarks whenever we dared enter the dining room. We much preferred to have our improvised meals in our own room.

I remember that on a certain *Shabbat* we stayed on the base. We were quite hungry. It had been a long time since we had been in the dining room to pick up a supply of food, and we had been eating the food sent to us in packages from home. I got up the nerve and went into the kitchen to get some food. Presenting a bold front, I entered by way of the back door. Two soldiers, busy washing dishes, paid no attention to me. I opened the bread pantry and took out a loaf of bread in a plastic wrapping. Then I took a package of cheese and a container of yogurt out of the refrigerator and turned around to make my exit. Passing through the door, carrying the supplies, I suddenly ran into the master sergeant.

"Hey, you!" he barked. "Hold it right there!"

I tried to run.

"You're a thief, a thief!" he shouted at the top of his voice.

I stopped and turned around, looking him straight in the face.

"I'm not a thief!" I screamed. "I just picked up some food because I'm hungry!"

I gave him the slip, running as fast as I could to my room in the women's barracks. The master sergeant did not make an issue of it. He must have understood.

The Army provided shallow, stereotyped popular "entertainment," presenting singers, one-act skits and various comedy and variety acts to lift the morale. Some of these performers were celebrities of the stage and screen who were idolized by the public. I could find no reason for admiring them. I found them pompous, self-important people whose fame had gone to their heads.

Our barracks were situated close to the landing strip, so that we knew exactly when the take-offs, landings and dog-fights were taking place. We sometimes witnessed the tragedies in which the airmen were involved. One day, we saw a burning fighter plane coming in for a landing. The flyer, an experienced fighter pilot, had been hit in a dogfight. When he noticed that his plane was aflame, he did not give up and bail out but managed to land the crippled plane, emerging from the wreckage, stunned and bewildered, but miraculously unscathed.

War is a crucible; it is a test that brings out the best and the worst in people. We witnessed many acts of pure unselfishness and heroism and, conversely, deeds that revealed deplorable human weaknesses and basic character flaws.

In 1970, the war of attrition ended, and the cease-fire went into effect. We breathed a sigh of relief. The mental tension eased, but the pressures of the job continued unabated. I had a feeling that this was only a lull between battles, a feeling that proved to be accurate with the outbreak of the Yom Kippur War three years later.

Occasionally, I would leave the base to sit down on one of the sand dunes. Around me the endless desert extended in perfect tranquility, but I sensed that the serenity was deceptive. Sunset in the desert appeared like a huge blazing flame, fanned by whispering winds. It was an awesome sight.

I wanted to run away, but I knew that we were fighting for our existence, that we were fighting a war from which there was no escape. I knew that if we would win the war, both sides would live. But, God forbid, if we were to lose, we could not hope to survive as individuals or as a nation. I wanted to flee, to get away from the sand, the battles, the memories and the specter of death hanging over us. But there was no way out. A hidden and indefinable power had determined that I should be there.

Disappointment

*I*n connection with my work for the Air Force, I did a lot of flying to all parts of the country, seeing different places and meeting different people. My horizon broadened, and I realized that when I would be discharged from the service, life would never be the same again for me.

My friendship with Judy and Chavah, however, remained unchanged. The girls would listen with utter fascination to my experiences in the Air Force, and to me they represented a link to my sheltered and carefree life of the past.

One evening, while I was back in the *kibbutz* on a two-week furlough, we decided to take a trip to Eilat and Sharm-el-Sheikh at the southern tip of the Sinai. The way we planned it, Chavah and Judy would leave for Eilat on Sunday, and I would fly on an Air Force plane to Sharm-el-Sheikh on Thursday where we would meet and hike into the desert for a few days.

On Thursday afternoon, I arrived at Sharm-el-Sheikh by plane, exactly as scheduled. When I went to the place we had agreed to meet, the girls were not there. I searched for them all over the place, I even inquired at the police station, but the girls had not been seen anywhere. I decided to go to Eilat, one hundred twenty miles to the north of Sharm-el-Sheikh, to look for them there. Since I had no money, the only way for me to get to Eilat was to find a kind person with whom I could hitch a ride. I stationed myself at the military checkpoint on the road leading out of Sharm-el-Sheikh, hoping to catch a ride. After a short while, a civilian van stopped. The driver, a man in his fifties, agreed to take me along. The guard at the barricade, noticing my misgivings about joining the man, put my mind at ease.

"I know this man," he said reassuringly. "He is the local contractor who is putting up the residential buildings here in Sharm-el-Sheikh. He's all right."

"Hop in," my host said with a smile. "I can take you all the way to Eilat."

That night I slept on the beach in Eilat, and early the next morning I began my search for Chavah and Judy.

My search for the girls produced nothing at all. They simply were not there. I did run into three volunteer workers from New Zealand whom I knew from the *kibbutz*. They had not seen the girls. The police station could not offer any help either.

That night, I slept on the beach again, and in the morning I decided to return home. I managed to hitch a ride with an elderly couple in a small blue Volkswagen who took me as far as Yerushalayim. From there, it was not a difficult thing to get back to the *kibbutz*.

When I arrived I found Chavah and Judy waiting for me.

"What happened?" I asked. "Why weren't you waiting for me in Sharm-el-Sheikh on Thursday?"

"We never made it to Sharm-el-Sheikh," Judy said. "Tuesday night, after we got to Eilat, we slept on the beach. We really enjoyed the new experience of sleeping out on the soft warm sand. The next morning, we heard that they were shooting scenes for a film and that they were looking for extras and bit-players. We just couldn't pass up an opportunity like this. We applied for the job and were hired on the spot. They put us to work on the set right away. That night, all the extras, who were mostly tourists, slept on the beach. There were two men who had a tent. They told us that the beach was crawling with thieves who steal the belongings of the people sleeping there at night. They suggested that everyone deposit their valuables in their tent and sleep lying in a circle around the tent. This way, we would be sure that no one took our things. When we woke up in the morning we discovered that the two men had absconded along with the tent and all our belongings. Luckily we still had enough money to buy a bus ticket back to the *kibbutz*. So now you know why we did not show up in Sharm-el-Sheikh."

We all had a hearty laugh, but in my heart I felt sorry for them.

The end of my two-year stint in the Army was rapidly approaching. I was looking forward to going back to civilian life, but at the same time I was worried. The Army had been a kind of refuge for me, an environment where decisions were made for me, where all doubts were removed, where every day was planned, where your life had a purpose, that of protecting your country. All this was coming to an end. It was scary.

The day of my discharge arrived. I said good-bye to my girl

friends at the base, Sarit, Leylah and Tamar. All the girls from the women's barracks prepared a farewell get-together. I told them I was going to miss them, and I really meant it. They had become part of my life. I took off my uniform and changed into civilian clothes. Then I returned to the *kibbutz*.

The discharge from the service was supposed to make me happy, but instead, it turned out to be a source of great concern. What was I going to do with my life? I really should be setting goals for myself and making plans for the future. I suddenly found myself confronted with a bewildering multitude of options. I had to make the choices and decisions myself. No one was going to do it for me.

I returned to the *kibbutz*. In the morning, I worked at doing odd jobs, or at what in *kibbutz* labor parlance is called being a pinchhitter. My spare time I spent listening to music, reading or chatting with friends.

It all happened so suddenly. My discharge from the Army created a void that cried out to be filled. My ties to the past were disintegrating. My best friend Chavah told me that she was planning to emigrate to the United States. The news did not come as a total surprise to me. I always suspected that Chavah's professed love of Eretz Yisrael and her maudlin yearning for her homeland were nothing more than echoing the empty cliches of our leftist educational system, without any inner commitment.

While in the service, she had met an American fellow, a computer analyst, who was working as a consultant for the Israeli Armed Forces. Within the brief span of a few weeks, Chavah settled her affairs in Eretz Yisrael and moved to Los Angeles where she got married and raised a family.

Shortly after my discharge, my American friend Judy

returned to Cincinnati. Life on the leftist *kibbutz* which had seemed so romantic and appealing at first, left her with an emptiness inside and did not satisfy her yearning for spiritual fulfillment.

I felt lonesome and forlorn, stuck in a rut from which there seemed to be no escape.

Volunteer Work

*T*he departure of Chavah and Judy created a void in my life. I spent hours in solitude, staying away from company, avoiding contact with friends. To distract my thoughts I took on the arduous job of taking care of the flower beds and the shrubbery and other gardening chores in the *kibbutz*. From early morning, I was busy tilling the soil, weeding, pruning, raking and cultivating. Coming to my room after work, I would flop into bed. At night, I studied. I decided to pass the matriculation exams, and with that in mind, I bought books and study guides to prepare myself for the tests. After a few weeks of intensive study I came through beyond my fondest dreams. During these months of hard work, I developed tough muscles and a beautiful tan.

It was around this time that I was asked to help out for a few weeks in a small *kibbutz*. The *kibbutz* was situated in the Ezor Hameshulash, the "Triangle Zone," a predominantly Arab region in northern Israel. Always ready for a new challenge, I went there and was assigned to managing the kitchen. Aided by two volunteer helpers, I prepared the meals for two hundred people each day. One of the volunteers working in this *kibbutz* was a tall, robust fellow by the name of Sammy who hailed from San Francisco. One day, my curiosity got the better of me.

"Tell me, Sammy," I asked, "how is it that you came to work in this *kibbutz*?"

"Let me explain," Sammy replied. "You see, when my grandfather passed away last year he left me a large fortune. I simply didn't know what to do with all that money, so I decided to pack my satchel and go see the world. And that's how I wound up in this place."

One bright morning, Sammy asked me to come along with him on a hike to the neighboring Arab village. I hesitated. I was not sure whether it was safe for us to walk around unprotected in an Arab village. But Sammy put my fears to rest.

"You've got nothing to worry about," he said, flexing his powerful biceps. "I'll take care of you."

Against my better judgment, but relying on his physical strength, I agreed to join him.

In the afternoon, we entered the village to be met by a bunch of children howling at us in Arabic. Sammy looked at them and smiled.

"Cute kids," he said.

We continued on our way toward the village center. As we entered the narrow alleys, we noticed people closing the shutters on their windows. We did not think there was anything behind it. Suddenly, a rock came sailing through the air, aimed directly at us, then another and another. The "cute kids" were throwing rocks at us. Standing in groups of ten,

pitching their rocks from all directions, they had us trapped.
"Let's run," Sammy said, as he raced ahead. I followed,
running as hard as I could.

"I can't run so fast!" I screamed. "I'm not that strong!"

Sammy grabbed my hand, and dragging me behind him,
he raced at top speed. I felt as though I were gliding through
the air, my feet barely touching the ground.

The barrage of stones kept coming at us without letup. Big
rocks they were, each heavy enough to kill a man. I could not
understand how young boys were capable of hurling rocks
this size with such force. I figured that people were also
tossing rocks at us from the porches up above, and that was
where the big rocks were coming from. But I did not have a
chance to look up. Our thoughts were riveted on running, on
getting out of this village and into the fields as fast as our legs
would carry us.

The sun was setting when at last we found ourselves safely
in a field outside the village. We halted, completely out of
breath, gasping for air, huffing and puffing from the exertion
of running for our lives. We had no idea where we were. We
started to walk, hoping to reach the highway from where we
would find our way back to the *kibbutz*. After marching for
several hours, we arrived home late at night. Sammy was
visibly shaken by the experience. I said good night and went
to my room. That night I could not sleep a wink. The image of
the hate-filled children running after us throwing stones,
trying to kill us, pursued me. It reminded me of the pictures
I had seen of the holocaust.

Murder at the Airport

fter my discharge, I kept up a correspondence with my girlfriends from the Army. One day, I received an urgent message telling me that my friend Tamar had been hospitalized after being severely injured in an automobile accident. Without delay, I left work to travel to the hospital.

It seems that Tamar had taken her mother's car without permission and had gone to visit a friend who lived a distance away. En route, her car was hit by a truck. The car was totally demolished; she was lucky to come out of it alive. The truck driver, frightened and dismayed by the accident, took her to the hospital where she was being treated for multiple fractures. Tamar's father, a prominent public figure, was abroad together with her mother. Before leaving, he had warned Tamar not to drive her mother's car outside the city limits. Tamar, who had recently been discharged from the Army, promised but did not keep her word.

I was ushered into her hospital room and allowed a brief visit. As I left, I promised to come back the next day.

Arriving at the hospital the following day, I was denied permission to visit Tamar.

"Why can't I see her?" I asked apprehensively. "What has happened?"

"Haven't you heard?" one of the nurses replied, raising her eyebrows with surprise.

I became frightened.

"Please tell me what has happened," I pleaded.

"Tamar's mother has been killed," the nurse replied in a sorrowful tone. "She was murdered in the attack by the Japanese terrorist Kozo Okamoto at the airport in Lod. She was coming home after she found out that her daughter had been hurt in a collision with a truck."

I broke into tears. Death was at it again. What does a crazy Japanese have to do with Tamar's mother? What did she do to him? Why did he have to kill her and scores of others who just happened to be at the airport? How did it all come about? Who was responsible for this atrocity? When you come right down to it, she was killed for one reason only, the same reason for which my relatives were murdered in the holocaust. Because she was a Jew.

But what about Tamar?

"I must go and see her," I said to the nurse. "I promise I won't tell her a thing."

"All right," she replied. "But first you must calm down."

I entered the room. Tamar looked so small and pale against the large white bed. Her legs were in a huge cast, but she gave me a wan smile. My heart cringed with grief, but I had promised not to tell her. We chatted and joked as always. Not capable of keeping up the charade for very long, I left after a short while, promising to return.

"I know everything," Tamar said as I entered her room the next day. "They've told me."

At first, we sat in silence, then we talked a little. Coming back every day, I spent many hours with her in the hospital. Occasionally, the nurse would let me use an empty bed, and I spent the night out on the porch. Since Tamar's relatives did not feel comfortable visiting her after the terrible tragedy, I considered it my duty to be with her and not to abandon her during the distressing time she was going through.

Leaving the Kibbutz

A full year had gone by since my military discharge. I passed all the matriculation exams with straight A's. Tamar recovered and was released from the hospital. I decided to enroll in the university. I knew that I could not possibly pay the tuition fees, but I was confident that everything would work out somehow. I applied at several colleges and ended up choosing engineering as my major, primarily because I wanted to have a useful profession, one in which I could be productive. Tamar registered for a course in psychology.

For me, the most difficult thing turned out to be leaving the *kibbutz*. The *kibbutz* meant home and economic security. When you left the *kibbutz* you were, for all intents and purposes, a homeless person. Leaving the *kibbutz* is not the same as changing apartments or moving from one city to another. A person leaving the *kibbutz* is considered a defector, and he is shunned like a renegade. The *kibbutz* will never come to his aid. Even his parents cannot offer him any help, for they are dependent on the good will of the *kibbutz*.

Leaving the *kibbutz* was a frightening step for me to take; I would be completely on my own, without financial security and ostracized by the society in which I had grown up. But there were other things to consider, such as my aversion to go along with the leftist doctrines of the *kibbutz* and my inability to conform to the socialist mores of the *kibbutz*. These factors tipped the scale.

I always knew that I was going to leave the *kibbutz* at the first opportunity, in spite of my fears of having to stand on my own feet, facing deprivation and uncertainty. I was happy to turn my back on a way of life I did not believe in. I did not know what represented the truth or what was right; but I was sure that under no circumstances was I going to spend the rest of my life in a *kibbutz*, in a place where I had no freedom to decide how I was going to lead my life. In the *kibbutz*, I was forced to choose Marxism and Leninism and abide by any decision that was arrived at by the majority. The majority dictated every issue and every public and private aspect of life. My total disgust with this system outweighed all my fears and concerns about loss of comfort and security.

I cleared my room in the *kibbutz*, rented a room in the city and immersed myself in my studies. In the afternoon, I would do odd jobs, and my parents helped me a little. I was hoping to begin a new life, to advance in my studies and to find a true partner in life. I wanted to marry a man with good qualities, a person whom I could cherish and on whom I could depend. I remembered my grandmother's admonition "to find a decent boy from a respectable family." Once I would find him, she assured me, everything else would fall into place. Truly a sound piece of advice. I was very lonely in the big city. Poverty and loneliness forced me to devote myself entirely to my studies and my work.

I adjusted very well to the college environment and to my class; most of the students were men, and there were only four girls taking the course. One of these, a bright and charming girl, became a close friend of mine. The things that upset me most were the embarrassing shortage of money, the loneliness and being away from my family. It was the combination of all these factors, but above all the loneliness, that motivated me to seek a life partner.

In my class, there was a young man who on the surface seemed to be quite unassuming, but who had certain qualities that I liked. He was well-mannered, gracious, soft-spoken and considerate. A brilliant student who stood out above the rest, he was neither boastful nor conceited. I never heard him ridicule anyone or hurt anyone's feelings. I recognized his noble character and admired him greatly for it. We became acquainted, but he considered me as a casual acquaintance and nothing more. His name was Uzi.

One fine spring day, Uzi invited me to come along with him to watch the military parade, staged for the Independence Day celebrations, in Yerushalayim. I was surprised, but I gladly accepted. On the way to Yerushalayim we had time to talk.

"I've been meaning to tell you something important that's been on my mind for a long time," Uzi broached the subject, "but I've never gotten around to it."

"Okay, I'm listening," I answered laconically, although my heart was pounding.

Uzi's little Fiat seemed to become even smaller in the mammoth traffic jam we were caught in that extended all the way to Yerushalayim.

"I have a very special feeling for you," Uzi continued. "To me you are a lot more than a study partner. I don't know if you feel the same way about me, but it seems as if we shared the same destiny, as if we were meant for each other."

I felt a shiver going up and down my spine. Those were beautiful words, but all I was able to answer was a bland, "Huh, really?"

"You must think I am a cold fish," Uzi replied, "a bookworm without feelings."

How wrong he was. I was overcome with emotion, but I was tongue-tied like a shy little girl.

"You want to know something?" I blurted out. "I think you're very nice."

What had become of all my lyric phrases, my imagery, my metaphors, my polished prose?

We never made it to the parade; we were stuck in traffic all afternoon. Uzi turned off the highway and returned to his parents' house. His words were still ringing in my ears, but then I thought, how can I be sure he's the right one? At any rate, I was happy to be in the same class with him. This would allow me the opportunity to evaluate his character.

A Trip Abroad

*T*he semester was coming to a close. The dean announced that five students from our class had been selected to participate in a work-study program in a foreign country during summer vacation. Two students were slated to go to the United States and three to England. I could hardly believe my ears when he read from the list that Uzi and I had been chosen to go to England. How did this come about? What hand was guiding our wheel of fortune? We were very excited. Evidently, Uzi's hunch was correct; we did share a common destiny.

The friendship between Uzi and myself continued to blossom, reaching the point where we both realized that it was more than mere camaraderie, that it was affection that joined our souls.

A few weeks later, we flew to England to participate in an advanced course organized by a well-known British organization.

On the night of our arrival in London, I wanted to watch the sunset over the big city. I approached the desk clerk of the hotel where we were staying.

"Could you tell me at what time the sun sets in London?" I asked timidly.

"Don't worry, lady," he reassured me with his dry British sense of humor. "I promise you, the sun is going to set."

I was dispatched to work on a project in a charming town in the south of England, in the Devon region. Uzi was sent to work on a major project in northern England, in a town near Sheffield. We spoke on the telephone a great deal, talking about our experiences.

After work, I enjoyed going out into the meadows, into the greening little hills and walking along the cow paths amidst a rich tapestry of colorful wild flowers. What a welcome contrast to the arid barrenness of the Sinai Desert! The late nightfall in England made it possible for me to do a lot of hiking. I would sit down on the banks of a small stream and watch the swiftly flowing water. Entranced by the soothing sound of the swirling current, I would be inspired to write a poem.

Whenever I felt lonesome I would call Uzi. Occasionally, we would meet on a weekend; there was always so much to talk about. We truly enjoyed each other's company. The months of working on the various projects were coming to an end, and we still had four weeks until the beginning of the new semester. Moshe, one of the students in our group, was doing work in London. We put our heads together and decided to rent a van and go on a sightseeing tour through Europe. Moshe rented the van; we met in London and set out on a journey that took us to Scotland, Belgium, Germany, Denmark, Holland, France and Switzerland. We were planning to catch the plane in Zurich to fly home.

Moshe was a mystery to me. He grew up in a religious home, and one day he solemnly declared that, as a result of something that had happened to him on our trip through Europe, he had decided to do *teshuvah*. He got up early every morning, put on a *tallit* and *tefillin* and prayed from a small book he carried in his briefcase. He cautioned us that his utensils were kosher and not to be used for meat dishes; they could be used only for dairy dishes. It sounded very strange to me.

"I know that Hashem exists," he said emphatically, "and I have to pray to Him."

We did not enter into a debate with him, but while he was away and without his knowledge, we inadvertently made his utensils *treif*. Many years later, when both Uzi and I began to observe Torah and *mitzvot*, this sin weighed heavily on my conscience.

One of the most thrilling experiences on our tour was being able to pass freely from one country into another. Peace without barriers or border lines! All our lives we had known only war. We were accustomed to being surrounded by enemies bent on our destruction. Moving in and out of countries without restraint, sometimes even without having to show a passport, left us openmouthed and thunderstruck. It was a fabulous feeling. Another thing that impressed us to no end was the abundance of water, especially in Scotland, the land of blue lakes. In Israel we have only one small lake, and we lovingly call it Yam Kinneret, "the Harp-Shaped Sea," and in Scotland we found a countryside dotted with hundreds of vast lakes brimming with pure water.

Our last stop in France was Lyons, where we arrived on the day before *Yom Kippur*, October 1973. We stayed with a friend

of Uzi's who was studying there. Moshe went to the synagogue. Uzi was feeling under the weather, and I thought he
was running a fever. I prepared a cup of tea for him, and he
went to sleep.

Early the next morning, Moshe went again to the synagogue, and we stayed in the apartment. Uzi turned on the
radio, and suddenly we heard some familiar words and
names. Uzi, who knew a little French, listened intently.

"That's it!" he burst out. "There's a war going on in Israel!"

Occasionally, the music was interrupted, and we were
able to recognize a few words in the newscaster's tense-
sounding report; words like *guerre* (French for war), Israel,
Egypt, Syria.

The Yom Kippur War had broken out.

Uzi jumped out of bed.

"We've got to get going," he said calmly, but firmly. "Let's
drive over to the synagogue to pick up Moshe, and from there
we'll go straight to Zurich. We have to go home."

I quickly packed my bags. Although Uzi was burning with
fever, he drove to the synagogue. Moshe was shaken by the
news.

"It's war," he shouted. "We've got to get back as fast as we
can!" Uzi told him to take the wheel while he stretched out on
the back seat.

We drove all night, Moshe and Uzi taking turns at the
wheel. It all came back to me, the Sinai Desert, the sand dunes,
the deceptive silence. The war seemed so distant from the
tranquility of the peaceful, snow-capped Swiss Alps.

In the morning we stopped at a roadside restaurant where
we stilled our hunger with a plate of Italian pasta. We were
tired and worried. As we were driving we were trying to pick
up an English-speaking radio station to hear bits of news about

the events unfolding in Israel. Would we see our homes again? What was happening to our loved ones?

The Zurich airport was swarming with people. It was business as usual. Only the Israelis were running around anxiously from one department to the next. Scores of young men, attempting to fly back to Israel to join the war, were clustered in front of the El Al office. It was no use.

"There are no flights to Israel," the El Al spokesman announced. "The airport in Lod is closed to all foreign traffic. We did not even receive the daily newspapers from Israel."

Uzi was really sick. Clearly, even if there would be flights, he would be better off staying in Zurich until he recovered. Moshe was nervously pacing the floor.

"I have a suggestion," I said. "Let's all go to visit John."

John who lived in Zurich, had come as a volunteer to work on a *kibbutz*. He received us very warmly and treated us to a dairy meal with a selection of delectable Swiss cheeses. He and his family were very upset about the news reports coming from Israel. They told us about the sneak attack the Arabs had launched on Yom Kippur and that the fate of the Jews in Israel was still unclear. The general concensus was that we had to be prepared for the worst. The news was bad, the situation grave.

Another holocaust, I said to myself. Death takes no furlough. Why is this happening? Why is there no letup in the incessant killing of Jews? All the lame arguments the Arabs are offering are nothing but excuses for killing Jews.

The mystery remained unsolved.

We spent the rest of the day at the Zurich airport, hoping for a resumption of the flights to Israel. After a couple of days, the El Al office announced that they were preparing to initiate flights for men who were serving in combat units. Moshe reported for duty at once and registered for the flight. Uzi, who was still in pain and running a high fever, decided to stay until he recovered. Moshe departed the same day and we a few days later.

As we were approaching the coast of Israel, the tension in the plane became palpable. Two Mirage fighters came in our direction and flew alongside of us until we landed at Lod airport. The ground was shrouded in darkness. The lights in Tel Aviv were blacked out as were the lights of the airport. After the chilly weather of Switzerland, the heat in Israel felt oppressive. The terminal in Lod was virtually empty, and the few arriving passengers hurriedly gathered up their belongings. Uzi received orders to join his unit in the Sinai at once. He was granted permission to say good-bye to his parents and pick up his uniform at home. It was late at night. His parents were anxiously waiting for him. I came along with him to his parents' house. I knew it would be a painful and protracted farewell. The fighting was still raging, and no one could predict the outcome.

We said good-bye. Early in the morning, Uzi left for the Sinai Desert.

Body and Soul

*T*he winter sun shining brightly in the deep-blue sky gently caressed the dormant earth. Small puffs of white clouds, like a flock of young lambs, dotted the wide expanse. Trees were gleaming with a soft tinge of green after a week of tempestuous rains. The howling winds had subsided, and the birds were celebrating with joyous song. It was one of those rare beautiful mornings in the rainy season, and I was in a jubilant mood, for this afternoon Uzi was coming back. The whole world was smiling.

Three months had gone by since the outbreak of the Yom Kippur War. Uzi was still serving in the reserves, somewhere in the Sinai Desert. We had not seen each other for a long time, and I was eagerly looking forward to his return. The previous night he called to let me know he was coming. It was a glorious day in more ways than one, a dazzling, thrilling, exhilarating day.

Classes at the university resumed routinely in the new semester, although there were many empty seats, since a number of students were still in the service. In the morning, I had a few free hours between sessions, and I used the time to take private dancing lessons from Nicole Shemer in Tel Aviv. When I arrived at her studio that morning, Nicole, as always, greeted me with a friendly smile. She started off with a workout in posture and balancing on the parallel bars and proceeded with dancing exercises. I looked dreamily out the sunlit window, reflecting on why time was creeping so slowly, wondering why every minute seemed like an hour. Mrs. Shemer asked me why I was so absentminded. She was satisfied with my answer but did not ease up on the exercises.

At long last the lesson was over. I left feeling relieved, happy for each second that was ticking away. Mrs. Shemer came along with me, and we walked down Rothschild Avenue together, enjoying the clean streets and the invigorating pure air after the drenching rain. A sense of gladness filled the atmosphere.

At the corner, we parted and went our separate ways. I turned into Benzion Avenue, walking toward King George Street. It was a typical Tel Aviv morning rush hour. The aroma of fresh rolls and the bracing fragrance of fresh-brewed coffee pervaded the downtown air. People were rushing in all directions, each wrapped up in his own private little world.

Mindful of Nicole's admonition on the importance of poise and posture, I walked with confidence, holding myself straight as a pencil. I was wearing the comfortable leather boots my mother had brought me from Italy and a pink woolen dress she had knitted for me. Although it was quite chilly, I did not find it necessary to wear a coat. I was carrying a briefcase with some notebooks and personal articles.

I was thinking of Uzi who would be arriving later in the afternoon, glad that we would see each other again after so many weeks.

I turned into Bograchov Street. Ahead of me I had to pass the skeleton of a new building under construction. The sidewalk was torn up, piles of sand covered the area, and there were pieces of wood and other debris scattered about. A short way up the street a big woman with curly blond hair approached.

Then it happened. Suddenly, I felt a violent blow strike my head. I fell flat on the ground in front of the big woman. A heavy eighteen-foot wooden beam, plunging from the scaffold atop the five-story structure, hit me and sailed into the street as if thrown by a catapult.

Given the height of the building, the impact of the force of gravity and the fragility of my skull, it was a miracle that I was still alive.

All at once, I felt I was outside my body, floating upward about twelve to fifteen feet above the sidewalk, watching the scene below. I did not know how I left my body, or how I got up there. Everything happened so suddenly that I was caught completely by surprise. I saw the big woman bending over my body, trying to detect a sign of life in my motionless form. Then she started screaming for help. Several passersby stopped and stared at my body. Reacting to the insistent cries of the woman, the people became alarmed and deliberated as to what to do.

The woman, still kneeling beside me, looked up.

"Where's the building contractor?" she yelled. "Where's the foreman on this job?"

The other people joined in the shouting.

On the roof, a young man emerged.

"What's going on down there?" he shouted. "What's all the commotion?"

The woman pointed at my body.

"I want to speak to the building contractor this minute!" she insisted.

The young man disappeared, returning a short while later.

"The contractor is up here," he said. "He won't come down, and he won't talk to anyone."

I could see my body stretched out on the sidewalk.

This is my body, I thought, but I am not inside it. I am looking at it from above. How is this possible? With what eyes am I seeing this, and where are my ears? How could I be hearing all this noise in the street?

It was strange to look at myself from the outside, knowing with certainty that this was my body. I was viewing it from a different perspective, since while I was inside my form I could not see it from the outside. Now I was looking at my body the way I used to look at other people. I was baffled. Obviously, I existed, I was real, I was conscious, but not inside my frame. I always thought that "I" and my body were identical. I did not know that I was a being that was more than just a physical body.

I was not at all afraid. Quite the contrary, I felt fine. I felt no pain or bruising; I felt relaxed, buoyant, worry-free. I existed independently of my bodily functions. I did not need any physical organs to see, to hear or to think. All the while, my body was lying dead-still on the sidewalk, unable to function without my presence. All its faculties were now with me, outside my body, hence, my flesh-and-bone frame was unable to react or move. I was observing it from my external vantage point. When I was inside my body I saw with my physical eyes; now I perceived without them, and they—my eyes of flesh—saw nothing.

My sense of vision, thus, existed even without my physical eyes; the ability to reason existed even outside my brain. All my life, I had seen by means of my eyes, heard by means of my ears, reasoned by means of my brain. My consciousness had been fully integrated with my body into one inseparable unit. But now everything was different. Being separated from my body was an amazing, supernatural experience. I was surveying the scene from above, looking not only at other people but at myself, at my own material body.

A gradual change began to occur in my status of "observer." The events in the street began to fade away into darkness, and through this darkness, I perceived a glimmer of brightness. As the radiance came closer it grew in intensity, becoming a glorious, powerful light, radiating an abundant flow of exalted spirituality.

In harmony with this flow of illumination, the events in my life began to pass before my eyes. The images were three-dimensional, and I saw myself taking part in them. My entire life flashed by, from the day I was born until the very moment I fell to the ground.

The vision I saw was like a wide-screen film in which I had the starring role and was also the audience. The images streaked by very rapidly, yet not a single detail was omitted. It was like a video on which every incident is recorded, every musical note, every shade and color that enhanced my life, and now everything was being played back at high speed and with astounding sharpness. I do not remember the actual vision I saw. What endures in my memory is my surprise at the amazing vividness of the images, recalling long forgotten events and details. I wondered where this visual memory was coming from. How did I suddenly remember my entire infancy and childhood? These questions cropped up as I was watching the replay of my life. When the vision ended I asked myself whether it had really been my own life. I came to the conclusion that indeed it had been. The entire experience filled me with an indescribable sense of exalted happiness.

Once again, I saw the blinding luminescence, glowing in a soft velvety white, as if an infinite number of brightly flashing magic sparks were uniting in a burst of spectacular brilliance. I tried to compare this brilliant glow to the colors of light from various sources I had seen when I was inside my body, but even sunlight paled in comparison to this awesome superabundance of immeasurable brightness.

The magnificent stream of light was accompanied by a flow of sublime love, a kind of love I had never before experienced. It was unlike the love of parents toward their children, the love of friends and relatives or the love of Eretz Yisrael. Any love I had ever felt was nothing but a tiny speck compared to this exalted, powerful love. Even if all the sparks of love that abound in this world were to combine they could not equal the powerful, pure love I sensed.

Faced with this overpowering love, I felt incapable of remaining an independent entity; I simply melted away. I was too small to withstand the flow of goodness streaming toward me and into me. I tried to defend myself, to close my eyes, but I had no eyes to close! I had no way of hiding before the radiance. I had no body. I felt completely stripped of the outer shell that had protected me in this world. There was no possibility of evading the current of love that enwrapped me. No words can describe the enchantment, the wonder, the incomparable, infinite goodness. I discerned in it qualities of compassion, spiritual pleasure, strength, happiness and beauty, all in infinite profusion.

I was powerless. I had no way of expressing myself. My body was lying on the sidewalk, totally incapacitated.

I felt my very being dissolving. I knew that if I did not return to my body immediately it would be too late; my mortal being would cease to exist. I realized that the only reality was the reality of this light, the essence that prevails beyond the physical world. I thought, how can there be a "self" inside a body? How can a person have self-awareness? The instant I was swept up in the wonderful light, my "self," my "I," dissolved into nothingness. Any sense of independence, pride, anger and desire vanished. All selfish tendencies disappeared, since my ego was about to be absorbed into the great light.

I felt a powerful bond with this marvelous presence. This was the will of a higher Power, a Being of infinite might. I felt a strong pull to become part of this wonderful eternal flow. It attracted me like a magnet with the power of its goodness, just as the earth exerts its attraction on the physical body. This magnetic force consisted of a confluence of goodness, light, faith, pleasure, self-effacement, joy, love, compassion, beauty, hope and favor that drew me closer with its overwhelming magnetism.

Filled with awe and reverence I turned to the wonderful Being and told Him about the extraordinary attraction He wielded over me.

"I am drawn to following my inclination," I said, "but I ask to be returned to my body. I ask to be given another opportunity in this world."

I went on to relate about Uzi, about the long time we had not seen each other because of the war, about our devotion to each other, about the meeting that was slated for this afternoon. I resisted the attraction of the Higher Will. I asked Him not to separate us. I told Him about my doubts and my search for the truth, until I had found Uzi and knew that he was truly meant for me, about my feeling that we were one, heart and soul.

I had a sensation as if I were being torn away from Uzi, just like you rip up a piece of cloth or paper. It felt as though my soul was being torn away from his soul. My "I" and Uzi's "I" were in reality one and the same "I" that was being forcibly shattered. I was surprised that I had not felt this way toward any of my relatives and friends. I knew then why I had met Uzi and why we were together. I knew that we were essentially one single indivisible being.

My body and all I had done with it, that is to say, my life in the physical world, were described to me in the third person. There appeared before me a young woman who lived her life the way she was brought up, and I—meaning my soul—was not this woman. I was not the body that had been living in this world. Never before did I feel like this. I always saw myself as one personality, a fusion of body and spirit. Only now did I realize that my body and I were two distinctly different entities that have been united in this world for a certain purpose.

Looking at myself, I was overcome by a depressing thought.

Too bad, I thought. She was so young and did not have a chance to live a meaningful life.

The accident happened on my birthday. I was thinking about this young woman of twenty-two years of age whose lifeless body was lying in the street. I reviewed her/my life, a life without any real accomplishment. I felt as though I was waking up from a dream, the dream of my life. For the life I was living had flitted away; nothing was left of it. I sensed that I had not fulfilled my task in life, I knew that I had pursued false objectives. I understood that my soul had come down into my body to fulfill a certain assignment. I did not know what this assignment was, but I knew it had not been carried out. I was disappointed that the purpose of my life had not been accomplished.

The wondrous light did not interfere with my feelings and thoughts or influence them in any way. It was simply there; the absolute truth. It did not impose any demands on me, nor did it take responsibility regarding the purpose of my life. The light was simply present in my inner consciousness, an integral part of my feelings. It did not tell me the true meaning of life, what was its purpose or why I resided inside my body all those years. It did not express any judgment regarding my actions of the past, whether they were good or bad. But simply by being there, surrounded by the light, I intuitively knew with absolute certainty that I had not fulfilled the mission for which I had been joined with my body in the corporeal world, in the *olam haasiah*, the world of action.

I was overcome with a deep sense of regret for the time I had wasted. The time I had received as a gift had been frittered away without being put to good use. It became clear to me that presently, being outside my body, I could not do anything in the world of action. Becoming an integral part of the marvelous light did not ease the distressing feeling that I had squandered my life. I felt sorry for my body which had been my faithful companion, the body which I should have elevated but did not. I sensed that I had used my body improperly, and I wanted to set a new course for my life.

I was gripped by a powerful desire to come back and live a true life. I asked to return into my body that was sprawled on the street, to return to my loved ones, to life itself. I knew that only inside the body, in this world, can the will of the One

Above be made real.

The pull of the powerful love of the benevolent light was almost irresistible. I felt my willpower crumbling and melting away. I knew that if I would not go back this very instant, I would not want to or be able to return any more. I would not be able to return, because I was losing my "self," my identity, my yearning to return to my body. Faced by this outpouring of goodness and love, I was losing my will to be a separate individual. It felt as though a loving mother embraced my individuality and pulled my "I" toward a state of perfect happiness, toward an elevated state of being that ensured everlasting sublime delight. I was filled with great compassion for my loved ones who would remain in this world, for my body, for the life I had wasted. A wave of pity swept over me.

I felt that this force of compassion brought me back into my body. Overcome with tenderness, with a boundless sense of compassion, I burst into tears. The big woman bent over me, and grabbing my hand, she coaxed me to get back on my feet.

My soul returned to my body. I made it back. I do not know how I re-entered my body; everything happened so fast, and before I knew it, I had slipped back.

Return to Reality

*M*y body was shuddering with fright, shaken by the traumatic upheaval. It was only with great difficulty, and with overwhelming fear and convulsive spasms, that it managed to retain me within it. My body was capable of getting up off the ground and standing unsteadily, but it was unable to express "me." It seemed as though we had not yet been firmly reattached.

I looked up, gazing at the sun with my physical eyes. How pale the sun looked! How limited was its power to radiate heat and light. Ordinarily, going out into the street on a bright day I would wear large dark sunglasses to protect my eyes from the blinding sunlight. Yet here I was standing without sunglasses, looking straight into the sun and finding it rather dim.

I suddenly realized that the light of the sun actually protects us, protects our body, shelters the corporeal existence of *olam hazeh*, of this world. The light of the sun conceals the supreme light. I recognized that if this wondrous light were

to illuminate our *olam hazeh,* our material world, I could not
have remained inside my body. I would have left my body and
never returned. I knew that our existence here is only a
semblance of the true reality of the wonder of the infinite
light.

I was reminded of the story I had read as a child about the
"invisible man," a man who would drink a potion that had the
power to make him invisible. He saw everything that was
happening around him, but no one could see him. This would
enable him to be helpful and do favors for people in need. I
thought that this infinite light was something akin to the
"invisible man." It is an existing reality, a life-giving force that
moves and guides the world, yet the world cannot see this
infinite light. Nevertheless, people can sense instinctively
that it exists. If this glorious light would shine on our world we
could not survive in its overpowering brightness.

My body was shaking with uncontrollable fits of sobbing,
while I, still partially detached from my body, felt an ethereal
happiness. I was fully conscious and completely aware of the
condition of my body, as if I was still observing it from above,
only this time I was inside my body. I wondered whether my
weeping was the same as the wails of a baby that could not talk.
My mood was certainly the exact opposite of crying; I was
happy, my mind was remarkably alert and clear, my compre-
hension superb, and I was enjoying the prospect of meeting
Uzi in the afternoon.

I felt unspeakably happy about having been granted a new
lease on life. I had been given another chance. I knew it was
a miracle, a personal miracle that happens only very rarely. I
looked at the heavy beam that had hit me, as it was lying there
on the pavement.

Why, of all things, did it have to be a beam that struck my

head? Why was it not something else that caused my soul to depart my body? Everything that happens is determined by *hashgachah pratis*, Hashem's close supervision of each person; you might call it Divine Providence. This I came to understand fourteen years later, when I read the essay entitled *Bati Legani* ("I Have Come to My Garden") by the Lubavitcher Rebbe.

This is what the Rebbe says: We can draw down the *Shechinah*, the Divine Presence, into this world, into the *olam hazeh*, so that Hashem will dwell among us. This can be accomplished if we turn darkness into light. The Torah writes, in connection with the *mishkan*, the tabernacle, *ve'asita et hakerashim lamishkan*, "Make upright beams for the tabernacle." (*Shemot* 26:15) The word *keresh*, "beam," is comprised of the same letters (*kuf, reish, shin*) as *sheker*, "lie" (*shin, kuf, reish*). When you build the tabernacle, you transform the *sheker* of the world into *keresh*, beams, the components of the Sanctuary. Hashem pledges that this will result in *veshachanti betocham*, "I will dwell among them." (*Shemot* 25:8)

The Rebbe goes on to explain that *sheker* also contains the same letters as *kesher* (*kuf, shin, reish*), meaning, "bond, connection." In order to cause Hashem to dwell among us, we must serve Him, not by a process of monastic withdrawal from the everyday world, but rather by being involved and connected with the world. Through our involvement with the world we will transform the world into a place of *kedushah*, holiness, turning darkness into light.

My body was shaking convulsively, unable to produce even a single word. At this stage I did reside again in body, but I realized that I was not an integral part of it. My body got up, stood erect, wept, reacted to any command I issued, but my power of speech was gone. It was then that I became aware of the strong alliance that existed between me and my body. I realized that my body was a tool, an instrument, my trusted partner here in *olam hazeh*. I, that is to say, my soul, could act, express itself, create and elevate itself only by means of the body.

From that day on, I stopped abusing my body. I stopped smoking, overtaxing my body by staying up late, eating harmful foods and losing my temper. Many years later, I read the words of *Chazal*, our Sages, *"Keilim na'im marchivim daato shel adam*. Beautiful utensils give a person contentment."* (*Berachot* 57a) I recognized that in a metaphorical sense this refers to the utensils the *neshamah*, the soul, uses. The utensils of the soul are our body and the spoken word; these should be beautiful, unblemished and filled with *mitzvot* and *maasim tovim*, good deeds.

I do not know how long I was outside my body. Perhaps it was only seconds, possibly minutes or more. Everything happened beyond the confines of time, transcending the limits of time. In the place where I had been, time had no meaning; the concept of time did not apply. Down here, in the street, only a few seconds or minutes had elapsed, since by the time I returned to my body, people were still screaming for the contractor on the roof to come down. A gallant young man resolutely walked over to the stairway.

"If the contractor isn't coming down," he shouted angrily, "I'm going up to get him."

The threat worked. The young fellow on the roof called down that the boss was coming in.

A few minutes passed. The people around me were perplexed that I had not spoken a word. I just seemed to react to what they were saying. The big woman excitedly grabbed me by my arm.

"Listen to me," she said in a voice trembling with emotion.

"This *Shabbat* you must go to the synagogue and say *Birkat Hagomel*. This is the thanksgiving blessing that is said by a person who has survived a dangerous situation."

I gratefully agreed, but in my heart I wondered what kind of blessing this was, and where I could find a synagogue in my neighborhood.

As a child I had visited a synagogue on one single occasion. It was in the neighborhood where my aunt lived, and it had been on *Simchat Torah*. All I can remember from that visit is a handful of candy, a bunch of children running around and men carrying an object wrapped in a cloth mantle that had a crown on top. The men were trying to sing without much success. The synagogue was located in a run-down shack. I was astonished that the woman had told me to go to a synagogue. I had been taught in the *kibbutz* that only backward people went to a synagogue, people who were afraid to confront life, and that in a synagogue they perform strange and irrational ceremonies.

The woman continued to talk to me intensely.

"You have to sue the contractor," she insisted. "He's responsible. Don't let him get away with this."

She gathered up my belongings, which were scattered all over the sidewalk, and put them back into my briefcase. On a slip of paper, she wrote the address of an attorney on Allenby Street.

At this point, a heated argument erupted between the building contractor who was coming down the stairs and the young man who was threatening him.

"You'd better see to it that this young woman gets to a hospital right away," the young man demanded, the people nodding in agreement.

"I'll do no such thing," the contractor protested. "She

seems to be in perfect shape."

While this discussion was going on, I continued to cry, unable to utter one word. I felt sorry for the building contractor. He looked pathetic. A short man with a wrinkled face, about fifty years of age, he was wearing a hard hat and worn-out work clothes that were hanging loosely over his scrawny frame. Perched precariously on the tip of his nose was a pair of thick glasses through which he peered as he spoke. He was a sight.

The man looked around impassively, stupefied, and dazed. It seemed as though the entire incident did not concern him. Evidently, the beam had accidentally slipped out of his hands. The entire construction site was a shambles, lacking even the most elementary safety precautions. I could not understand what prompted a man like this to put up a building. He looked as if he did not even have the desire to live.

The big woman raised her voice, trying to shake the man out of his stupor and his apparent indifference, and I continued to cry. He looked at me sheepishly, then stared at the beam lying in the street. Suddenly, he turned toward the passing cars and tried to hail a cab, waving his hand vigorously. The people, noting that I was being cared for, began to disperse. Only a few of them waited around helplessly, questioning the contractor about how this accident had happened.

The big woman who had lifted me from the ground also remained with me and did not stop talking. The contractor then asked all the others to go about their business. He led me to the busy King George Street, hoping to find a cab there. I followed him, crying bitterly. He tried to calm me and implored me to stop crying, but I was unable to stop, just as I was incapable of speaking.

"I promise you," he said soothingly, "everything will turn

out all right. Just stop crying, won't you, please?"

I knew that everything was going to be fine. After all, I was going to see Uzi this afternoon. Did I need more? But I could not explain anything. The contractor kept dragging me along, trying in vain to hail a taxi. It was no use. At last we arrived on foot at the Samenhof Clinic.

The contractor approached the receptionist and told her about the accident. She directed us to the X-ray department, where the contractor related all the details. After completing a form, he tried again to speak to me. The nurse handed me the forms, asking me to fill in the details for the X-ray. The contractor, who gave up speaking to me, wrote his name on a piece of paper and handed it to me. He then found a seat for me on a bench in the waiting area in front of the X-ray room. The people waiting there looked with surprise at the incongruous sight of a middle-aged builder taking care of a crying girl.

"She's been involved in an accident," he explained. "She received a heavy blow to her head. Could someone get her a drink of water, please?"

With that, he turned and left.

I waited my turn to enter the X-ray room, weeping incessantly. There were about twenty people ahead of me.

"How about letting her go in ahead of us?" one of the men said. All the others nodded in agreement. Evidently, they could not bear seeing me cry.

After a brief discussion, a young woman with dark wavy hair and sparkling dark eyes came over to me.

"You may go in next," she said. "Everyone agrees to let you go ahead."

I was unable to say anything, but I smiled gratefully at the kindhearted people.

The results of the X-ray were good. My condition was absolutely normal, and my head showed no signs of injury. I was overwhelmed by the miracle of it, by the amazing discovery that my head had remained intact after the blow it had absorbed. Since everything appeared to be all right, the doctor sent me home. I was in no mood to go to class, and I decided to go home to rest. I did not have enough money for a cab, so I decided to take a bus.

Coming Back to Life

C heerfully, I stepped out into the street. Things had never looked quite as rosy as today. The air was fresh and stimulating, and my body was whole. The images around me seemed uncommonly sharp and clear. The world seemed different somehow from before. People around me were busy and rushing about, their faces expressing unhappiness and discontent.

Everything seemed so bizarre, like a city of phantoms. Why don't they recognize the truth? Why do people live in misery, and without hope? It seemed as though they were all looking down at the ground, each fretting about his troubles. Why don't they lift their eyes toward the sun, toward the universe, toward the beauty of creation? I could not understand why people do not burst into song, into a mighty song of thanksgiving for the privilege of walking this earth. Why don't they show others the truth, the wondrous eternal light, the joy of creation, and point out to them that there is a spiritual world beyond the limits of the physical universe?

I knew I could not adequately describe this other reality. I recognized that my vocabulary was capable only of expressing finite concepts, that it was unequal to conveying the totality of the supernal perfection that transcends the confines of the material world.

The world seemed to me like a gigantic crystal ball, a glass house whose walls are one-way mirrors, so that you can look in from the outside but the occupants cannot look out. People seemed to be locked up in their private worlds, each inside a circle that was placed around him, as if everyone was programmed to act a certain way, as if everyone was unalterably bound by the cycle of his destiny, unaware that he had the potential of breaking out of the entanglement and crossing over into another circle. It seemed as if everyone was groping in the dark, unaware that there was a light switch. Many years later, I came across a description that resembled this feeling when I read Rashi's commentary on the plague of darkness that Hashem brought upon the Egyptians.

Was I the only person who ever experienced "the other side"? Were there other people who are aware of the Existence that envelopes the cosmos, the Essence that is the source of all being, the Almighty Who is concealed while He reveals Himself? It did not make sense that I, a simple woman with no special qualifications, should know something that no one else knew.

From a rational point of view, my out-of-body experience could not have happened, yet I was certain that it was no hallucination. I was also sure that I had not gone insane, that I was in my right mind. Proof of this are the ensuing years of my life which I lived in complete normalcy.

I had no doubt that there were other people who had had

similar out-of-body experiences and knew about the existence of the exalted infinite light. Where could I find them? I found the answer after a search that lasted for many years. After seven years of fumbling in the dark, I established the connection with the light.

In the meantime, my condition was peculiar. On the outside, I was crying, while in my heart, I was happy. I was like the sad clown who makes everyone laugh but who is himself weeping. Only with me the situation was reversed. I was laughing, and my body was grieving.

I was surprised that I was able to walk the streets after the horrifying incident, capable of entering the bus and paying the fare. The people gawked at my tear-swollen eyes, but this did not bother me in the least. I had come back to life.

Late in the afternoon, I arrived home. My crying spell ended. I felt no pain. In an inexplicable way, everything was bright and cheerful, and I felt euphoric.

I prepared a cup of hot tea. I was in no mood to eat solid food. I lay down on my bed and tried to relax. I sipped some tea and tried to organize my thoughts. Uzi was supposed to arrive shortly. I could hardly wait to see him again. The clock seemed to be standing still. I called Mrs. Shemer, my dance instructor, and managed to tell her about the accident. I described to her the beam that had struck me, the terrible blow that had landed on my head, the events that happened afterwards in the street, my plodding along with the building contractor, the X-ray and my return home. She was shocked and made me swear to go to bed immediately and not to go out for an entire week. She described to me the severe damage the brain can suffer as a result of moving around after a concussion of this kind.

"You are totally irresponsible," she chided me. "You

should have been hospitalized and undergone a complete physical."

"They won't believe my story," I retorted. "The contractor left me in the Samenhof Clinic and then disappeared. And besides, I have no symptoms whatsoever, and I feel no pain."

Nicole Shemer was not impressed. She explained to me that the symptoms would appear later, and the pain, too, would eventually make itself felt. Finally, she said that she was canceling my lessons until we knew with certainty what my condition was. She added that she was coming over to spend the night with me, to make sure that I was all right.

My euphoria did not last long. My talk with Nicole Shemer brought me back to reality. I understood that I had a serious problem and that I had to be careful. At this stage, I did not want to notify my parents; I wanted to spare them the worrying. I stayed in bed, waiting to hear from Uzi. I dozed off until the phone rang. It was Uzi. Excitedly, I told him about the accident, explaining to him that Mrs. Shemer was on her way over and would be staying for the night. He replied that he would first go to his parents' house.

"I'll come over to see you in about an hour," he said in a cheery voice.

Seeing Uzi Again

*H*earing his voice as he entered the door, my heart skipped a beat. Even today, tears well up in my eyes when I think back to this moment. This was not merely a meeting of two friends who had been separated; this was a meeting of friends who have returned from the dead. *Baruch Hashem*, Uzi came back from the war unscathed, and I came back from another world, the *Olam Ha'elyon*, the World Above. Although nearly twenty years have passed since then, I still vividly feel this sense of parting and meeting again. Every time we go to work in the morning, or when we say good-bye on other occasions, I am accustomed to walking him to the door or to the car and watch him as he disappears in the distance. And every time he comes home after work or after a trip, I thank *Hakadosh Baruch Hu* that we were privileged to meet and to build a truly Jewish home filled with warmth and caring, where we can bestow kindness on each other and fulfill the Will of Hashem in the physical world.

Uzi entered and sat down on a chair next to the bed, his eyes reflecting deep anxiety. Mrs. Shemer, who had arrived in the meantime, stayed in the background as I told Uzi all the details of the accident. I also described to him the out-of-body experience I had. He was stunned. Neither of us had ever heard anything like this before. We had no understanding of what had happened, where I had been or what I had seen. Intuitively, both of us felt that I had returned from apparent death. Beyond that, we were unable to explain anything.

Uzi agreed with Mrs. Shemer that I should stay in bed for the time being.

"Please call your parents," he insisted, "and let them know what happened. I have to return to my base tomorrow morning. Mrs. Shemer is kind enough to stay with you tonight, but someone should be with you all the time."

We decided to keep my out-of-body experience to ourselves and not to reveal it to anyone. We were convinced that I was sane and rational, and we knew if the story were to become common knowledge there was the risk that someone might want to have me committed to an insane asylum. I told the story only seven years later, after studies on OBE's (out-of-body experiences) had been published by Dr. Elizabeth Kovler-Ross and Dr. Raymond Moody, *Life after Life*, Mockingbird Books, 1975.

The question may be asked: If this Higher World is so exceptionally beautiful, why did I want to return into my body? Why, in fact, does a normal person want to live in the first place?

For an ordinary person, there is a simple answer. *Hakadosh Baruch Hu* has implanted into nature the urge to live, a most powerful urge. We all want to live, and we don't know why. Many people live a life of misery, pain, poverty and disease, or they undergo difficult trials and tribulations, yet of their own free will and choice, they all want to live. Only very few decide to commit suicide; they are the exceptions. On the surface you may think that this will to live stems from the fear of the unknown after death, the belief that after death there is nothing but emptiness or an overpowering love of wordly pleasures, such as eating, drinking, sleeping, entertainment and the like.

However, since I found myself in an idyllic, perfect state, why did I want to go back to this life? There are several answers to this question. First of all, there were my yearnings for the companionship of a soul that was very dear to me. Then there was the distress I felt over not having conducted my life properly. Granted, I breathed, ate, slept and had served in the Army, but such a life did not count, it was of no consequence. Another reason for my delight in returning to my body was knowing that now I would begin to lead a truly meaningful life, emulating the Divine qualities of love, helping others and enjoying *simchah*, spiritual joy.

Today I recognize that I must give thanks for each day and each minute that I can fulfill the will of the Creator as it is expressed in the Torah. I do this by overcoming the *yetzer hara*, the evil tendency, by attempting to banish sadness and despair and by being filled with the spirit of joy and hope.

The Baal Hatanya (Rabbi Shneur Zalman of Liadi) defines this struggle as a war against the body which the *Gemara* characterizes as an *ir ketanah*, "a little city," which is besieged by "a great king," the *yetzer hara*. Present in the city was a poor wise man, the *yetzer hatov*, who saved the city with his wisdom, which is symbolic of *teshuvah* and good deeds. Happiness abounds when you feel that your soul is in control of your body and directs it to do its bidding. By subduing your feelings of anger, hate, jealousy and revenge you uplift your soul. You conquer the *yetzer hara* by showing kindness to other people, by recognizing the Divine spark that is present in all of Creation.

There are misguided people who attempt to commit suicide. What foolishness, what delusion, what missed opportunity and what a waste! This is due only to the fact that they think that the world has no guiding spirit, that they control their own destiny. They believe that they are ending their lives. The truth is exactly the opposite: they are putting an end to the cycle of life that is governed by Hashem's *midat harachamim*, the attribute of compassion. They forget that *Chazal* state, "Never abandon hope for Divine compassion!"

We have seen people trapped in the most difficult situations whom Hashem extricated and led from darkness to light because they set aside their personal calculations and had complete faith in Him.

Commenting on the verse "I shall not die, but I shall live" (*Tehillim* 118:17), Rabbi Yitzchak of Vorki said, "You must first blot out yourself, eliminate your selfish tendencies. Only then will you be able to live the true life. Once you have done this, you realize that you don't have to die, but that you will really live."

Migraine Headaches

I decided to stay in bed for a while. I did not leave my apartment, although initially I felt fine, except for a mild headache. On the third day after the accident, I noticed a peculiar change. My forehead began to swell and slowly turn blue. Fingering my head, I discovered a slight bulge. Gradually, my headaches intensified.

One day, to my dismay, I discovered a bald spot on the back of my head. Little by little, the symptoms of an apparent hemorrhage spread over my entire face. First my forehead, then my eyes and cheeks and finally my entire head and neck became swollen and turned blue. Beneath my eyes I had two black circles that made me look like a ghost. People were horrified looking at me.

I began to have nightmares. Irrational fears took hold of me, especially after dark. I would lie in bed, staring at the walls and ceiling, scared to death. I explained to myself that these phobias were groundless, but my imagination was running wild, painting frightening shadows while eerie sounds echoed inside my head.

Having company was the only remedy for these nightly fits of anxiety; whenever I had visitors the fears would subside.

I began to develop a method to combat this new "buddy" of mine. During the day, I had ample time to think of ways to master him. The technique I used was to keep this "buddy" a secret, known only to me, and not reveal his presence to other people.

Whenever the phobia would emerge I would attack it with rational and convincing arguments and cause it to disappear, along with all the bizarre creatures it was conjuring up. After a few months, I conquered my fears. They never came back.

During this time, Uzi called me every day, and after a week went by, he urged me to go to stay with my parents. I did not want to tell them about my condition, but I felt I had no choice. I called my mother, and within less than twenty-four hours, a *kibbutz* vehicle pulled up to take me to my parents.

When my mother saw me she was appalled. My puffed up blue face and the two black bags beneath my deep-set eyes certainly did nothing to enhance my charm and beauty.

My parents really pampered me. The day after my arrival I was taken to the hospital in style by ambulance to undergo a series of tests in the neurology department. The doctor gave me a thorough examination, and the results were satisfactory. He told me that I showed a slight lack of coordination (the correlation between the commands given by the brain and their execution by the limbs), but that it was not serious. He also found that my sense of balance was slightly impaired.

The doctor was interested to learn more about the accident, and when I told him about the heavy beam that had dropped on my head from the fifth floor, he flashed a benign smile.

"That's impossible," he chuckled, leaning back in his chair. "You must be exaggerating. Nobody receives a blow of that magnitude and lives to tell about it."

He ordered me to stay in bed for at least another week and wrote a prescription to relieve the headaches.

I stayed with my parents for two more weeks. My face was still blue, but it was a lighter shade, and the puffiness began to subside. I decided to go back to college.

Uzi was discharged from the service just when I began to feel better, and we both resumed our studies. He returned home feeling tired and sick. The tension of the war and the tough life in the service had taken their toll. He developed a painful stomach ulcer. For me, attending the college classes turned into an ordeal of interminable misery. I would sit in class, and when the lecture was over, I could not remember anything. My fellow students could not understand how my personality had changed so drastically. When they were talking to me or asked me for something I would instantly forget what they were talking about, so that they had to start all over again. I failed most of my tests.

Sometimes, I would promise to do things for people, and a minute later, I would have no recollection of it. These episodes of amnesia often resulted in a chain reaction of unpleasant and embarrassing incidents. People would become furious at me, and I, in turn, would respond indignantly or break down in tears. Cigarette smoke would give me severe headaches that virtually paralyzed me so that I could hardly breathe. As a result, I constantly became embroiled in arguments with people who were smoking in my vicinity. I felt that they were insensitive to me.

My headaches became so acute that sometimes I woke up in the middle of the night and cried for hours. I took aspirin, but it was totally ineffective; the throbbing pain persisted relentlessly. I could feel how it affected different areas of my brain. The headaches brought on bouts of nausea and made me shiver all over my body. The pain was excruciating. I could not go out without a hat. If I did go out bareheaded in the sun, I would have an agonizing migraine attack within minutes. I was careful to wear a hat all the time.

Finally, I decided to go see a doctor. He examined me and referred me to a neurologist. The neurologist had a rather strange look about him. He was a lanky, gray-haired elderly man, wearing thick glasses. I noticed that he had a nervous twitch in his face and hands, which raised serious misgivings in my mind about his competence. He asked me various questions about what I had seen during the accident and whether I had perceived any unusual sensations, but I did not tell him anything of what I had experienced. I was afraid that if I told him about the wondrous light I would be committed to the psychiatric ward. I just spoke in generalities. The neurologist then gave me a superficial check-up and prescribed a strong medication for my migraine headaches.

As soon as I left his office, I threw away the prescription. I realized that I had to conquer the pain by myself, without any sedatives or tranquilizers. Today, I know that I was right. With the passing years the headaches abated to the point that they became more or less tolerable. I recognized that if I were to become addicted to medication the pain would never leave me.

Subsequently, I visited two other nerve specialists, making sure to take all available tests, so that there would be no doubt that everything was all right. Except for a few mild disturbances, no further episodes of any significance occurred, and I was diagnosed as suffering a ten to fifteen percent permanent disability. Every doctor who examined me was amazed when I described the vehemence of the blow I received. They all agreed that it was impossible that I could have survived an impact of such magnitude.

And indeed it was a miracle that I had come out alive. I was positive that I was living only by dint of a *nes,* a miracle. The Hebrew word *nes* also denotes exaltation and elevation, as in the verse, "*Hashem nisi,* Hashem has raised me up." (*Shemot* 17:15) Thus, a *nes* is a phenomenon that transcends and rises above the laws of nature that Hashem has set for His world.

One day, the college dean summoned me to his office. For about half an hour, he reviewed and analyzed my scholastic record. Glancing at the spread sheets in front of him, he summed up his findings.

"I'm sorry to say," he declared, using his formal bureaucratic phraseology, "that on the basis of the grades you have been getting lately one must arrive at the inescapable conclusion that you cannot continue to study at this institution."

Looking up from the documents, the dean gazed at my distraught face that still showed some blue marks as if he now saw me for the first time in his life.

Suddenly, his voice took on a different tone, and his rigorous expression melted away, making way for a gentle smile. He explained that he himself had served for a long time in the reserves and had to deal with the problems of servicemen who were forced to interrupt their studies for many months. When I told him about my accident, he showed deep understanding for my condition.

"I'll do anything I can to help you," he said, rising from his chair.

After my interview with the dean, in spite of the reversal in his attitude, I almost lost all hope. I wanted to quit, but Uzi was not ready to give up. He insisted that I continue to try to get my diploma. I must admit that if it had not been for his encouragement and firmness I would not have been able to persevere. Thanks to his help and support, I eventually finished my studies and was awarded the degree I had my heart set on.

Another profound change came over me in the wake of the accident. I simply could no longer bear to watch any television broadcasts. Sitting in front of the set I would feel faint and suffer from splitting headaches that would bring me to tears. Television brought back the memory of the chagrin I had felt after the accident over the time I had wasted in *olam hazeh*, my existence on earth, instead of fulfilling the task I had to carry out in my life. My suffering was greatest when watching films depicting violence. I felt as though the television programs were controlling my thoughts and reactions. It seemed to me that the small screen blocked out "the other side," the spiritual world. I sensed that the message conveyed by television was untrue, a cunning deception and a fraud. To my mind, television was the antithesis of the truth.

Several months went by. The warm winds of spring were blowing across the land. I opened all my windows to let the pleasant air warm my chilled apartment. The fragrance of the blossoming trees that lined the avenue permeated the house. On the evening before Memorial Day, I was relaxing on the couch with a book when the doorbell rang. I answered the door, and before me stood the building contractor accompanied by a petite lady, his wife. I was surprised. Ever since the day of the accident—about four months earlier—I had not seen him or heard from him.

"How were you able to find me here?" I asked.

"I got your address from the police," he replied with a shrug.

I invited them to have a seat on the porch, wondering what this strange visit was all about.

The contractor spoke in a hesitant, almost monotone voice. "The reason we've come to see you is to ask you to drop the charges against us with the police."

With downcast eyes he went on to explain that their only son had been killed in the Yom Kippur War.

"In my present frame of mind," he sighed, "I could not possibly go through a court trial."

I felt sorry for them. What a tragedy!

I sympathized with them over the misfortune that had befallen them. They were so heartbroken. I tried to imagine what they must have gone through, but I simply could not put myself in their place. All of a sudden, I understood the reason for his behavior at the time of the accident, why he had abandoned me in the clinic, why he had not tried to inquire about my condition, why he had been so callous and indifferent about what happened to me. How could I be angry with a person who had suffered such a calamity?

I decided to drop the charges, and the case was closed, since no public charges had been brought against him.

Searching for Remedies

*T*ime marched on. Summer arrived. My headaches flared up persistently, and Uzi's painful ulcer continued to sap his strength. One of my friends, a young man named Binyamin, suggested a new cure-all for our aches and pains—meditation. Meditation would solve the problem of the headaches and the ulcer and would bring us inner peace.

A few days later, we joined a meditation class. We were initiated into the "technique" in a bizarre Indian ritual. We did not pay any attention to the ritual; all we were interested in was finding relief from our agonizing pain.

We began to practice meditation. Twice a day, we would sit motionless for a few minutes, like statues, in absolute silence. In our thoughts, we would have to hum a senseless *mantra* that went, *"Manga, ganga, inga, danga."*

Today we know that all these Indian cults and meditation routines are clever schemes concocted by Indian, Korean or other *gurus*. They use mind-control techniques to enrich themselves by entrapping thousands of unsuspecting young people.

Our futile search for a cure also led us to try to observe a vegetarian diet. This did bring about a marked improvement in our conditions. Due to the diet prescribed for us by Dr. Trainin of Yerushalayim, my headaches were in remission for about six months, and Uzi's stomach cramps disappeared altogether.

Another year went by. We finally completed our studies successfully and were awarded our college degrees. A cycle in our lives had come to a close. We now had a profession that would provide a basis for economic security. It was time to get married.

I had mixed feelings about the wedding ceremony. In the *kibbutz* people looked askance on any religious ceremony. Couples went through the motions of having a wedding merely to please their parents and relatives. It was considered a formality, bowing to social convention.

My *kibbutz* upbringing had taught me that the wedding ceremony had no meaning. Nevertheless, according to Israeli civil law I was required to arrange a religious wedding, otherwise we could not be registered as a married couple by the Ministry of the Interior. We thought it was ridiculous, but we felt we had to go through with it. Most couples in the *kibbutz* would go to the Office of the Rabbinate by themselves to get married, and several days later they would celebrate the *chatunah* with a sumptuous meal and dancing for invited guests.

At all the weddings to which I had been invited in the past, the banquet was always much more important than the wedding ceremony; during the ceremony, the relatives would gorge themselves and chatter, paying no attention at all to the *Kiddushin* proceedings. Therefore, we decided to invite only our closest relatives to the religious ceremony at the Office of the Rabbinate. The "*chatunah,*" that is to say, the festive banquet with all the invited guests, was going to take place two weeks later.

I had to set a date for the wedding, but first I had to have a consultation with the *rebbetzin* (the rabbi's wife) at the local Office of the Rabbinate.

The *rebbetzin* was a very lovable and charming lady. She was wearing an attractive head covering, her face reflecting true graciousness. Smiling benevolently, she explained to me the importance of marriage and the preparations that were required. I laughed inwardly but played along, listening carefully to the things she said without answering or asking questions.

She spoke to me about how to handle differences of opinion that might arise in married life, and I liked what she said. The intelligence and the wisdom of the *rebbetzin* genuinely surprised me. This was the first time in my life that I had spoken to a religious woman. In conclusion, the *rebbetzin* explained to me the importance of observing *taharat hamishpachah*, the laws of family purity. She told me that I had to immerse myself in the *mikveh* and show the certificate to the rabbi who would be performing the marriage ceremony. This was too much! Why do they force me to do something so weird, merely to be registered as a married woman? Having no alternative, however, I decided to go through even with the immersion in the *mikveh*.

On our wedding day, we both went to work in the morning as usual. To us, it definitely was an ordinary day. The wedding was set for six o'clock in the evening, which gave us enough time to finish our work, shower and change. We did not even bother to buy new clothes.

The ceremony took place in the wedding hall of the Rabbinate. It was very subdued and simple, with only our closest relatives in attendance. I had a very odd and peculiar feeling, yet at the same time I was gripped by a passionate fervor for which I had no rational explanation. The wedding ceremony held something uplifting that could not be explained logically. I was happy that we had decided to arrange the *chupah* this way, quietly, without inviting strangers. It imparted to the *chupah* ceremony a singularly private character and a sense of exaltation.

Today, many years later, I would define it as a moment of *kedushah*, holiness. Then I did not know this. I vividly recalled this feeling many years later. I had treasured it in my memory all that time.

Today, I know that marriage is the blending of two souls and forms the basis for bringing holy souls down to this world. It is for this reason that a Jewish marriage has the character of holiness and is called *Kiddushin*, sanctity.

Our Sages relate that in the Jewish way it is the man who looks for a wife and not the woman who looks for a husband. He is like a man who has lost something. Who does the searching? The one who lost the object searches for the object he lost. (*Kiddushin* 2b) The soul of the woman and the soul of the man are, in fact, one soul that descended into two separate bodies, and in marriage, the two parts of this soul are reunited. Marriage is not a random meeting of two strangers; it is ordained from Above.

In the Jewish view, the birth of a child does not happen simply by chance. At the moment of birth, a holy soul descends from the *Olam Ha'elyon*, the Higher World, to fulfill a certain assignment here on earth. The affection the parents have for each other determines what the character of this soul will be.

About two years after starting to practice meditation, we enrolled in a course in the principles on which this theory is based. The course turned out to be a complete surprise for us. At the introductory meeting we were told by the leader of the movement that we were about to enter a new age. He called it the "Age of Illumination." According to his explanation, this was the age in which the "Eternal Light" would come down and illuminate the world. We were astonished to hear that there was someone else who knew about the "Eternal Light."

At this point, meditation ceased to be a medical procedure for the relief of headaches. Instead, it became a religion, a philosophy of life, a doctrine according to which there were two worlds, a spiritual and a corporeal one. Man must strive to rise above the physical and attempt to achieve a state of absolute spiritual serenity, "to still the mind" and "eliminate distractions."

This state of mind, according to their view, could negate the material. For example, according to their theory, man can overcome the power of the earth's gravity and levitate; he can physically lift himself up and hover in the air by concentrating his thoughts. Another tenet of their philosophy is that nature has a personality of its own and controls the events in the world.

Over and over, I heard it said that man is controlled by nature; if "nature wants it" you can enjoy good health, if not, you must suffer illness. The only way you can rise above nature is by freeing yourself and attaining a stage of pure spirituality that enables you to subdue nature. Crying, according to their theory, is a sign of weakness. It is a symptom that proves that a person has not yet reached the "level of higher consciousness."

I was drawn to meditation because it was the first time I had come across a theory—spurious though it was—that explained existence beyond the realm of the physical. I had not yet discovered the truth.

The Meditation Settlement

D espite our interest, we never actually became members of the Institute of the Meditation Movement, and truthfully, because of our undisciplined ways, they did not think very highly of us. They resented our irregular attendance of the lectures, visiting only when it suited us.

After a period of about three years, we decided to establish our own settlement for meditators. This was going to be a settlement for supermen, a settlement without tension or fear of any kind, a residence for people who had conquered nature, an essence and life-style of a different sphere. For a number of years, Uzi had wanted to participate in building a new settlement and for me, it would afford the opportunity to investigate from close up whether meditational techniques were true or false. As long as we were living in the city I could not do this.

The settlement would provide the proof. We called it

Pisgit, from the word *pisgah*, meaning summit, peak.

The building of Pisgit progressed at a rapid pace. It was a fascinating pioneering experience, a story that could fill an entire book. Let me briefly try to describe how the settlement was erected and how it affected us personally.

In 1978, two years before the establishment of the settlement, we lived in Afula. One of our neighbors held a prominent position in the Jewish Agency, and through his intervention, we explored the possibilities of establishing a communal settlement to be underwritten by the Jewish Agency. However, our plan did not materialize.

One day, we heard from people involved in meditation that a group was being organized for the purpose of founding a settlement. This was our chance. We turned to our friends in the Agency requesting that they help us designate a suitable location to form the nucleus of the projected settlement. They suggested a number of locations in the Galilee and one location in Wadi Ara. After surveying the region and exploring the locations we decided to establish Pisgit in the Galilee.

We called a meeting of the initial settlers and told them all about the site. After making an inspection trip, they agreed to settle there.

We encountered opposition on the part of the Agency, since some of their officials argued that meditation was a cult and a religion. The truth is that we had no idea what religion meant, and we found these objections perfectly ludicrous. The way we were brought up was opposed to religion, and we certainly did not consider ourselves religious by any stretch of the imagination. We tried to convince the Agency that meditation was not a religion, that it was merely a simple technique for relieving tension. Luckily, the employees of the Agency did not know the meaning of religion either. Our efforts bore fruit, and our settlement was approved.

Having obtained the certification, we decided to start building, going up to the building site and joining the construction workers in building the homes. For months on end, we kept laboring, four people living on top of a mountain, without electric power, running water or sewage disposal. Occasionally, reinforcements would come to help out for a few days. We brought mattresses and slept on the floor in sleeping bags. A wooden board resting on old chairs served as a table. It was a marvelous experience of living in the great outdoors, amidst the spectacular scenery of the Galilee.

We all lived in the same house, the only house that had walls and windows. We cooked in a communal kitchen. The Agency furnished a tank of water. Once a week, we would go down into the valley to buy food supplies.

Pisgit is situated on top of a craggy mountain in the central part of the Galilee, in a region famous for its enchanting scenery. The mountain is flanked by valleys. Looking in a northeasterly direction you can see the snow-capped peak of Mount Hermon, looking toward the west, the Mediterranean comes into view, toward the north, the mountain chain of the Upper Galilee, and toward the southeast the Yam Kinneret, the Sea of Galilee, could be seen. South of Pisgit is the Bet Hakerem Valley, which is dotted with Arab villages.

The stony mountain on whose peak Pisgit is situated reaches a high altitude and is buffetted by fierce winds. In the winter, we would wake up in the morning and look down the slopes to find the valleys below covered with a cotton-like blanket of clouds that ringed the mountain in a gentle embrace. Sometimes, the clouds would rest on top of the mountain enveloping us in a thick fog. For several days, visibility would be limited to ten or fifteen feet. Walking inside a cloud was a unique experience, as phantom-like figures suddenly appear in front of you, only to vanish an instant later. It was like walking in the dark or like walking inside a tangible substance. I felt as though nothing existed in the world besides me and this cloud, and I was walking inside it. It reminded me of playing hide-and-seek when we were children, feeling safe and secure in the hiding place I had found. The mountain was like a gigantic creature with a life of its own.

At night, the view was even more enthralling. Tens of thousands of tiny lights glistened like diamonds in the valleys and on the distant mountains. Since we had no electricity and were wrapped in total darkness, the sight was even more fascinating. We loved to walk by the light of the moon and gaze at the marvelous spectacle. When the electricity was hooked up and the settlement was illuminated, the nightly enchantment faded somewhat.

After a few months, the homes were completed and the first families began to arrive. It was an undertaking that demanded a great deal of self-sacrifice. Families with small children and little babies arrived at the settlement with all their belongings in the very dead of winter, and we did not even have a telephone. Electricity was produced by means of an Agency generator that would break down from time to time, and our water came from the big reservoir in the center of the settlement. There were occasions when we would run out of water and were forced to wait for a new supply. At a later stage, a pipeline was laid across the mountains, but it was a disappointment; often the pump would malfunction, or one of our Arab neighbors would slash the pipeline.

We did very hard physical work, the kind of labor we were not used to. But we derived much satisfaction from having the privilege to build a *yishuv*, settlement, in Eretz Yisrael. After the construction was completed, I went back to my job, working as an industrial engineer in the North.

By this time, the phobias that plagued me after the accident disappeared completely. My fears were replaced with a strong faith, a belief in the "Great Light" that protected me wherever I went. In connection with my work, I had to drive over desolate roads a distance of about one hundred miles every day. Sometimes, I would stay overnight in a small Druze village nestled in the Upper Galilee. I was not afraid of anything. I would travel alone without concern, day or night, on the remote roads of the Galilee, fully convinced that the "Great Light" was everywhere.

I was also involved in setting up industrial projects in the Galilee district. One night, it was about nine o'clock and I was on my way home from work. My car came to a sudden halt; the motor went dead. As much as I tried, I could not get the engine started. To my dismay, I noticed that my car had broken down in the middle of a large Arab settlement in the Bet Hakerem Valley. About one hundred and fifty feet ahead of me I noticed a large house. As I entered I was met by a group of men and women who greeted me with a friendly *"Ahalan vesahalan."*

"My car broke down up the road, not far from your house," I explained. "A mechanic will come in the morning to get it started. Would someone please take me to the police station?"

One of the people drove me in his car to the police station. I said good-bye to him, thanking him profusely and wishing him well.

In the police station, I encountered two young police officers with guns strapped to their belts. It was already ten o'clock.

"There's no way for me to get to Pisgit," I explained. "It is

more than ten miles away from here, and there is no telephone
up there yet. Would you please take me home in your police
car?"

They seemed frightened and confused.

"I'm on duty here tonight," the shorter one explained,
"and I'm not allowed to leave my post."

"It's very dangerous travelling the mountain roads at
night," the taller one tried to convince me.

All my reasoning met with stubborn refusal; nothing
could convince them. I was at my wits' end.

"You've got nothing to worry about," I said as a last resort.
"After all, I'm travelling along with you."

"That's true," the taller one replied. "But on the way back
I'll have to travel alone."

"Don't worry," I reassured him. "Midway up the mountain there lives a nice Bedouin family who will be happy to
help you if, God forbid, something happens. There have been
times when I was forced to climb to Pisgit on foot, and they
always received me graciously."

He looked at me as if he did not believe me. Then he began
to feel embarrassed. He, a policeman carrying a gun, was
afraid, while I, a woman without a weapon, showed no fear
at all. Apparently, this was what convinced him, for he agreed
to drive me to Pisgit in the police jeep.

One day, a friend of an acquaintance of ours, a fellow by
the name of Yuval, proposed that we help him build a stand
at a fair being held in Haifa. In return, he would pay us a
percentage of his sales. The fair lasted for several nights, and
each night after closing, we would relax and talk over a cup of
coffee at a nearby coffee shop.

One night, the conversation turned to the subject of the

holocaust. Whenever I happened to get involved in a discussion of this nature I was powerless to say anything. I felt that, psychologically, I could not deal with this topic. I was unable to confront the enormity of it. Yuval was not religious; he was not wearing a *yarmulka*. At first, I did not participate in the discussion, but listened attentively as Yuval spoke about *Hakadosh Baruch Hu*.

"*Hakadosh Baruch Hu* is the Supreme Power," Yuval explained. "We cannot see or touch Him, but it is He Who guides the world."

Feeling a surge of powerful emotion I was unable to contain my feelings.

"It does not make sense," I blurted out, "that an event so ghastly, an atrocity so heinous, a crime so unspeakably evil should have been planned by *Hakadosh Baruch Hu*."

Yuval gave me a somber and piercing look.

"How do you know what happened to those souls who perished in the holocaust?" he said in a deliberate tone. "Perhaps they were elevated and rewarded to an extent that we cannot possibly comprehend. Perhaps they are enjoying the Sublime good."

I was listening, but I did not answer. Tears were welling up in my eyes. I could not continue to talk about the holocaust. The subject stunned and stupefied me. I was choking, and I sensed an inner turmoil that reminded me of my accident. I could not answer Yuval, and in my imagination I relived the scene of seeing myself lying flat on my back in the street, far from the coffee house. I thought that the accident I had lived through appeared horrible to the onlookers, but in reality, it had meant only sheer goodness, and I was the only one who knew the full truth, who was aware of what really happened that morning.

I suddenly fathomed that Yuval's words contained a valuable lesson that I could apply to my accident. I learned from my accident that the things people judge to be evil are not always evil, and the things people judge to be good are not always good. I learned that my perception and my understanding were relative concepts, that I was incapable of seeing the totality of perfection inherent in an event, that I was unable to discern the good concealed in the things I considered evil, unable to detect the harm and the evil that sometimes is hidden beneath a thin veneer of good.

Breaking Away

O ur uplifting pioneer spirit began to wane with the arrival of the first families of the "meditation teachers." Their presence made us aware of additional defects in the meditation theory, and little by little, we came to the realization that meditation was not just a therapeutic technique but a religious cult. We had no idea what religion really meant, but we discovered that the philosophy they called transcendental meditation—TM for short—was in actuality a pagan religion of absolute egotism, a cult that worshiped the "self," that idolized selfishness and self-admiration under the guise of "self-development." We arrived at this conclusion after listening to lengthy discourses by these "teachers."

The first to infer this was Uzi. He refused to become "religious," surely not as an adherent of their kind of pseudo-religion. I still had my doubts and did not know what to make of the entire concept of religion.

135

In the end, I understood that Uzi was right. I felt I had been tricked and victimized. My high expectations of meditation were rudely dashed. I did not want to have any association with this idolatrous cult, primarily because its main principle was the worship of the ego. It was a heathen cult, based on the *avodah zarah* of the Vedas, the heathen Hindu scriptures of India, according to which each individual lives only for himself and "develops" himself to the point of becoming completely estranged from his fellow man. Everyone sits by himself for hours and hours, attempting to "enter quietly into the ethereal chambers of Creation," in order to transcend "nature which rules the world," to control this mysterious entity called nature and make it do his bidding. They preach that it is the task of the ego "to impose its will on the world," so that nature will serve the ego and fulfill the ego's desires. Many years later, I learned that this was the philosophy of Pharaoh in Egypt, who pridefully said, "My Nile is my own; I made it for myself." (*Yechezkel* 29:3)

I did not hesitate to express my opinion. To my amazement, no one tried to challenge me. As a result of our opposition, however, we were placed under a total ban on the pretext that we were radiating "negative vibrations," which are mysterious waves that interfere with the "development of the personality."

I had a mixture of contempt and compassion for the weakness of their so-called "creative intelligence." Our ban led to an ugly power struggle among the leaders of the Meditation Society with political infighting and intrigues. As for us, we turned our backs on the whole miserable lot and left.

To us, it was an exodus, leaving the darkness and entering into a great light. But our happiness was tempered with sadness, sadness over the souls groping in the dark that had been misled. We regretted that we were forced to leave the settlement we had worked so hard to build. We also felt sorry for the good friends who remained there. Nevertheless, our hearts were filled with great joy over the realization that we had passed another milestone on our road "going up to Bethel, the House of Hashem." (*Bereishit* 35:3)

A Shocking Discovery

*J*t was a sunny day in 1982, one of those lazy days in late August when the rays of the setting sun take on a gentler, softer hue. It was about a year after the establishment of Pisgit. We were still living in the settlement, but it was evident that it was not going to be for long. On this particular day, I had to go to Yerushalayim to take care of some business. I wore jeans, a short blouse and, of course, my famous hat.

Late in the afternoon, I called Esther, a childhood friend from my *kibbutz* years who lived in Yerushalayim, and she invited me to spend the night with her family. Esther had married Yehudah in the meantime and raised a family. We had not seen each other for a long time.

I arrived at their house early in the evening. We were thrilled to see each other again. We talked about our lives, and I told her about Pisgit. As we were talking, I noticed that Yehudah was wearing a small *yarmulka*. I expressed surprise.

"Well," he replied forthrightly, "I made up my mind to adopt the religious way of life."

We sat around the kitchen table, had dinner and talked late into the night. Yehudah and Esther were tired, and we decided to go to bed. I slept in the guest room on the second floor.

Before going upstairs, I noticed a book on the dining room table. Since I was an avid reader, I decided to read a little before going to sleep. I took the book and went up to my room.

I put my things in place, went to bed and picked up the book. The title on the cover read: *Siddur Tefillat Yesharim,* The Prayer of the Upright.

I started to read: "*Modeh ani lefanecha*—I gratefully thank You—*Melech chai vekayam*—O living and eternal King—*Shehechezarta bi nishmati bechemlah*—that You returned my soul within me with compassion—*rabbah emunatecha*—abundant is Your faithfulness!"

I was overwhelmed. I wanted to continue reading, and I realized at once that this book was unlike any other book I had ever read. This book I had to treat differently. Even the lettering was unusual. Some sections were in large print, while other parts were in smaller print. Occasionally, the type and the thickness of the letters alternated from normal type to boldface.

Very slowly, the images I had seen during the accident began to reappear in my mind's eye, as though emerging from a haze.

I continued reading: "*Elokai*—My Lord—*neshamah shenatata bi*—the soul You placed within me—*tehorah hi*—is pure—*ata beratah*—You created it—*ata yetzartah*—You formed it—*ata nefachta bi*—You breathed it into me—*ata meshamerah bekirbi*—You safeguard it within me—*ve'ata atid litelah mimeni*—and eventually You will take it from me—*ulehachazirah bi*—and restore it to me—*le'atid lavo*—in time to come."

My excitement soared. I had the urge to cry out, "That's right! I know that this is true!"

I wanted to tell people that I had personally experienced this. My soul was removed from my body, and it has been restored to it! But who would believe me? On the other hand, here it was, black on white, in the book that I had found on the dining room table, and obviously, people were reading it. What was going on here? Who had written this book? The questions kept coming in quick succession as I continued to read.

"As long as the soul is within me I gratefully thank You O God, my Lord, and the Lord of my forefathers, Master of all works, Lord of all souls—blessed are You, O God—Who restores souls to dead bodies."

At this point my emotions peaked. I was all choked up. Tears flowed freely down my cheeks. "Lord of all souls, Who restores souls to dead bodies . . ." The thing I dared not speak about for so many years was written here plainly and lucidly.

I was enthralled with the *siddur*. On and on I read without stopping, as if I were reading a suspenseful mystery novel. For about two hours, I read prayers and several chapters of *Tehillim*. While reading, tears were streaming from my eyes. I wanted to scream: "True! True! Whatever is written here is all true!"

I did not close my eyes all that night. Over and over, I browsed through the *siddur*, trying to digest in my mind what my eyes were reading. I realized that this was a book of commitment, of attachment to Hashem and communicating with the *Shechinah*, a book of supplications, assurances and commandments. I did not understand the meaning of these commandments and how they were associated with the Great Light, but I felt intuitively that by dint of these commandments an abundant flow of goodness and kindness is drawn down from Heaven to our world.

The tears that were flowing from my eyes reminded me of the uncontrollable crying spell I had had after the accident. Once again, I was weeping irrepressibly, although by nature I am quite unemotional and unsentimental. In fact, for many years I hardly cried at all. But these were tears of a different sort. I asked myself: How is it possible that for thirty years I had not even once read the *siddur*?

In the days ahead, there were many more surprises in store for me. Mainly on the following day, when I went to browse in the bookstores on Geulah Street which are packed with a rich variety of religious books.

That very same night I decided to observe *Shabbat*. I had no idea what *Shabbat* meant and what its observance entailed. The contrast between the socialist Saturday of the *kibbutz* and the *Shabbat Kodesh* reflected in the *siddur* was as sharp as the disparity that separates darkness from light. I inferred from reading the *siddur* that *Shabbat* was a state of spiritual elevation, a condition I had never experienced.

I was reminded of an article I had read about a boy who was born without an immune system to protect him against infectious diseases. The doctors were able to keep him alive for years inside a sterile plastic bubble which shielded him from bacteria. I thought about this boy whose entire life unfolded within the confines of this plastic bubble. He had no awareness of life in the outside world and did not know about cities, forests or the ocean. I, too, was living inside a "plastic bubble" called *olam hazeh*, the material world. I had no knowledge of the higher world that exists outside my corporeal "bubble."

Shabbat lifts one out of *olam hazeh*—the world of mundane concerns—and transports one into the sweetness of *me'ein olam haba*, a semblance of the World-to-Come. This higher world of *Shabbat* had been fashioned for the Jewish people according to a blueprint about which I knew nothing as yet.

Meanwhile, on that fateful night, I continued to read the pages of the siddur, following the prayers in their proper order. Over and over, I was struck by the wonder of it all.

"Let a person always be God-fearing privately and publicly, acknowledge the truth and speak the truth within his heart . . ."

The simplicity and clarity of the words struck a responsive chord in me. I needed no explanations or commentaries; it was all there before me in its literal meaning.

With growing interest I continued to read: "Master of all worlds! Not in the merit of our righteousness do we cast our supplication before You, but in the merit of Your abundant mercy. What are we? What is our life? What is our kindness? What is our righteousness? What is our salvation? What is our strength? What is our might? Are not all the heroes like nothing before You, the famous as if they had never existed, the wise as if devoid of wisdom and the perceptive as if devoid of intelligence? For most of their deeds are desolate and the days of their lives are empty before You, and the pre-eminence of man over beast is non-existent for all is vain. Except for the pure soul which will have to give an accounting before Your Throne of Glory."

Who, more than I, knows that a person will have to give a reckoning, that death is not emptiness and void? I remembered the scenes from the "film of my life" as they unfolded before my eyes when I was outside my body. I recalled my feeling of anguish and disappointment over my wasted life and my unfulfilled mission in this world.

I continued reading in the *siddur*: "But we are Your people, members of your covenant . . ."

Slowly, the recognition began to sink in that there is one nation in the world, a holy nation, a unique nation, a nation that recognizes the "Great Light"—Am Yisrael, the Nation of Israel, the Jewish people. I knew that I was a member of this nation, but I did not feel Jewish. I did not feel I had done anything to deserve this title. "Your people, members of Your covenant." But nonetheless, wonder of wonders, I am a Jewish woman. On my identity card it says: "Jew."

I read on: "Therefore, we are obliged to thank You, praise You, glorify You, bless, sanctify and give praise and thanks to Your Name. We are fortunate, how good is our portion, how pleasant our lot and how beautiful our heritage!"

I went over these words once more: "Our heritage." I was a Jew because of my heritage. But what was this heritage that made me Jewish? As much as I tried, I could not remember ever receiving any inheritance. But if this wonderful *siddur* states that we received a heritage then I am sure this heritage is in existence and all I must do is simply look for it.

The text continued: "We are fortunate for we come early and stay late, evening and morning, and proclaim twice each day: Hear, O Israel: God is our Lord, God is One."

Master of the Universe, how happy I was! Until now You were hidden, and now I have found You! Impulsively the words burst forth.

I went on: "Take to heart these instructions with which I charge you today."

I felt that this verse was speaking directly to me. I knew that it was my duty to do all these things, to bring them to fruition and to carry them out in practice.

I continued: "It was You before the world was created, it is You since the world was created. It is You in This World and it is You in the World to Come. It is You Who are God, our Lord, in heaven and on earth, and in the highest heavens. True, You are the first and You are the last and other than You there is no god. Fulfill for us, God, our Lord, what You have promised us. Give thanks to Hashem, declare His Name, make His acts known among the peoples. Sing to Him, make music to Him, speak of all His wonders. Glory in His holy Name, be glad of heart, you who seek Hashem. Search out Hashem and His might, seek His Presence always."

I thought back to the hours immediately after the accident, when I walked in the street thinking, Why aren't people singing and giving praise and thanks for the privilege of walking the earth? And here I was reading it!

I felt that my mind was opening up, as if I had been sitting in a dark room and someone suddenly turned on the light. For six long years, I had been searching, and now, in the seventh year I had finally found the answer. My tears were not only tears of joy; I also felt a sense of deep bitterness and self-reproach. Why? Why did I have to suffer so much? So many years of physical and mental anguish, years of wandering and searching. The best years of my life had passed by in hollow emptiness. They had turned to nothing, and yet this book, the *siddur*, was within easy reach. How many times had I passed a synagogue, yet it never occurred to me to enter! How many times did I visit a bookstore or a library, and not once did I come across a *siddur*? Why?

"Blessed are You, Hashem . . . Who forms light . . . He who illuminates the earth . . . with compassion . . ."

Is there anyone who understands as I do the intense

compassion with which the sun shines on this finite world of ours? Our finite body cannot absorb the radiant splendor of this Light. How great is Hashem's compassion when he restricts His essential infiniteness and withholds His endless light so the world may exist.

I reached the *Shemoneh Esrei*: "Hashem, open my lips, that my mouth may declare Your praise . . . You nourish the living with lovingkindness, You revive the dead with great compassion . . ."

It was this "great compassion" that brought me back into my body. I recalled the moment when my soul returned into my body and the abundant flow of mercy cascaded over me. I understood that it was through this stream of compassion that my life was granted me.

"You graciously give man discerning knowledge . . . Return us, our Father, to Your Torah . . . Forgive us, our Father, for we have sinned unintentionally . . . Please look at our affliction . . . Heal us, Hashem, and we will be healed . . . Bestow Your blessing upon us, O God, our Lord, this year . . . "

Everything in the world, all human affairs, are determined by Hashem. This we must acknowledge and affirm, that Hashem is the source of everything. The essence of sin is rooted in the false perception that man is the one who makes decisions, accomplishes, projects and charts his life. Does man determine where, when and into what family he is born? Does he decide when and how he will die? Does he influence how he will look and what his gender will be? Does he wield control over the state of his health? Does he bring his influence to bear on the social, economic and historic factors that affect his status in society? Why is it that precisely at the present moment everything is welling up inside of me and pouring forth effortlessly?

The ideology by which I was brought up preaches that we are masters of our own destiny, that we control our fate. The socialist philosophy of Hashomer Hatzair, therefore, causes its adherents to live their entire lives in mortal fear of the unknown darkness, the fear of death. This idea represents the blackest darkness and is a monstrous lie.

It takes massive courage and immense inner fortitude for anyone who was raised under this system to change his way of life and break his lifelong habits. He must rise above the scorn of the society in which he grew up and surmount the opposition he encounters on the part of his family. He must overcome personal attitudes and tendencies that have become ingrained in his character and uproot behavioral patterns that have become second nature to him.

I continued reading in the *siddur*. I read it and reread it, over and over. I did not believe what I was seeing. At long last I made it! I have come home! I felt like a girl who came back from captivity, like a girl who returned from drifting about aimlessly.

"O Guardian of Israel, protect the remnant of Israel, let not Israel be destroyed—those who proclaim, 'Hear, O Israel.'"

Indeed, there still is a remnant of survivors. Just a small remnant of Jewish souls who still know the essence of Israel.

I uttered this prayer to *Hakadosh Baruch Hu*: "Protect the remnant of Israel. We know not what to do—but our eyes are upon You . . ." We, souls within bodies, are at a stage that we do not know what is being done and we do not know what to do. We lift up our eyes and ask You for help. Therefore, "May Your kindness be upon us, Hashem, just as we awaited You."

A New Dawn

*T*he first blush of morning shone through my window. The faint glow of daybreak illuminated the sky, the first rays of a new day, the dawn of a different future. I knew that I had changed. I was certain that there was no turning back to the old ways. I understood that I was a daughter of the Jewish people, which made it incumbent upon me to do the things a Jew must do. Then and there, I committed myself to observing *Shabbat*, to entering into the spiritual environment that is called *Shabbat* and to becoming part of its essence.

I heard the children as they were waking up. I went downstairs. Esther was in the kitchen preparing breakfast.

"Good morning," she said, greeting me with a broad smile. She placed before me a plate of sweet-smelling Danish pastry and a cup of steaming hot milk.

The children were crowding around her. I slowly sipped the awful tasting warm milk while Yehudah returned from the synagogue and sat down with us in the kitchen.

"I've got something to tell you," I said. "I've been reading the *siddur* last night, and I got so excited, I simply could not fall asleep."

Their eyes registered genuine surprise.

"You should know that everything that is written in the *siddur* is absolutely true," I continued, my voice quivering with excitement. "You're probably wondering why I am saying this. You'll find out in a minute."

I told them all about my accident and the things that happened to me in the wake of it. The children became very quiet, everyone listening attentively. One could hear a pin drop in the sun-drenched kitchen as my tale poured forth and the panorama of events began to unfold. Never before did I relate my story to strangers, but somehow I sensed that here I was permitted to tell it.

When I ended, I noticed a mystified look on their faces. We had been the closest friends for so many years, yet I had never mentioned a word about any of this. Then Yehudah's expression changed to one of true delight, as if my story corroborated something he had been searching for. He told me about the research that had been conducted in the United States by Dr. Raymond Moody and Dr. Kovler-Ross in the area of out-of-body experiences (OBE) and near-death experiences (NDE) and their collection of reports of hundreds of cases of people who had experienced clinical death. They all reported experiences that conformed to the pattern I had encountered. Based on this documented evidence, the scientists concluded that there is life, or some sort of existence, after physical death.

I was very happy to hear this, since I did not want to be the only person in the world who had knowledge of an afterlife.

"What kind of light did you see?" Yehudah asked.

"I saw an essence, an existence beyond the physical realm of this world—the world of action—the world with which we are familiar."

Many years later, after having studied the Torah with its great commentaries, I realized that this essence of infinite goodness is the power that sustains the world in which we live. It is the essential reality that Avraham recognized. He comprehended the spiritual essence that is manifest "on the other side" of the physical world of time, space and gravity. He recognized the true reality of God and that our existence here is but a small fragment of the awesome Infinite Light, the *Or En Sof.*

"Did you actually see *Hakadosh Baruch Hu*?" Yehudah asked with childlike innocence.

Embarrassed by his question, I smiled.

"This is a hard question to answer," I replied. "I can only respond by saying yes and no."

"How's that?" Yehudah asked.

"I'm asking myself the same question," I replied. "I don't believe that I saw *Hakadosh Baruch Hu* in His true Essence. I know that's impossible. On the other hand, if one may say so, I apprehended a spiritual apparition that I could not have seen while inside my body, for the body cannot endure such an abundant measure of radiance. In the *siddur* it says, 'Bless Hashem, O my soul, O God, my Lord, You are very great; You are clothed in glory and majesty, wrapped in a robe of light, You unfurl the heavens like a curtain . . .' The 'robe of light' is the wondrous illumination that cloaks and conceals the Divine Essence. Perhaps what I saw was a semblance of this light. The overwhelming desire I felt to unite with this light proves that it is real, representing a sublime will. I might say that the light I saw was a manifestation of the Divine Presence with less than the usual concealment or with more than the usual openness.

"Let me give you an example that will illustrate what I'm trying to say. Think of the two concepts: speech and thought. When a person speaks he reveals his thoughts through his words. At the same time, he also conceals part of his thoughts. In other words, speech is not a complete reflection of thought. The speaker reveals a small fragment of his thoughts but conceals most of what he is thinking. So it is with the light. A little of it is revealed, but most of the spirituality remains hidden behind an impenetrable cloak."

"You mean to say," said Yehudah, "that you had the privilege of perceiving a degree of Godliness that is greater than what we can see? Yet you do not think you saw the Divine Essence?"

"Yes, you're right. But whatever it was I saw, it was much more than my soul could tolerate. That's why I felt as though I was dissolved into nothingness in the presence of this light. I could not contain this flow of plenty, much like a container that cannot hold more than its volume, and any overflow will spill. Since the dimensions of this wondrous light are infinite, the analogy of the container is not really applicable, for relative to the flow of plenty I felt as if I were non-existent."

Listening with deep interest, Yehudah continued to ask, "How can it be that this long story you are telling and the scenes you describe happened within the span of only a few seconds?"

"The location where I was while outside my body," I replied, "was in a dimension beyond the physical realm. It transcends time and space. I could perceive, experience and understand so many things in a brief moment of earth-time, because where I was, time has no meaning.

"In the same vein we can explain the concept of space. From what I told you, you get the impression that I travelled to a distant place, in the far reaches of the cosmos, a place light years removed from earth. In reality, I was in a supernatural domain, beyond the limits of space and time, a state where distance and place are meaningless terms.

"Since we are accustomed to thinking in terms of spatial and time-related functions it is difficult for us to understand how the space we occupy is, in reality, no space at all, and how all the worlds are in essence in the same place. When we speak of higher or lower worlds, we do not imply distance or elevation. We want to indicate that worlds are relatively closer to or farther removed from the Divine Essence."

Yehudah remained silent, immersed in thought. I, too, remained quiet. After a while, looking at Esther and me sitting across the table, he broke the silence.

"You gave me food for thought," he said with an enigmatic look. "It's very hard for us who are involved in the real world to understand such abstract and esoteric things."

"I agree with you," I answered. "That's why, when I read the *siddur*, I concluded that, in order to make my body a receptacle for *kedushah*, holiness, and the flow of plenty from Above, I have to change my way of life. I have made up my mind to observe *Shabbat*. Could you direct me to a place where I can buy a *siddur* and books about Torah laws and Torah views?"

Following his directions, I drove to Geulah Street in Yerushalayim and entered one of the religious book stores, wearing my jeans and blouse. This was the first time I encountered so many religious Jews wearing black coats and black hats. Although I was dressed the way I was, no one showed any resentment or glared at me. On the contrary, I never met people who were as kind and as friendly as these people. I glanced at the shelves and picked *sefarim* at random: *Mesillat Yesharim* by Rabbi Moshe Chaim Luzzatto, *Shaarei Teshuvah* by Rabbeinu Yonah, *Shemirat Shabbat Kehilchatah* by Rabbi Yehoshua Yeshayah Neuwirth, *Michtav Me'eliyahu* by Rabbi Eliyahu E. Dessler, *Gesher Hachayim* by Rabbi Yechiel Michel Tikuczinsky and, of course, a *siddur.*

The men in this store all wore black suits, white shirts and black hats or black *yarmulkas.* Their faces reflected a special inner tranquility, and they all behaved in a dignified and unassuming manner, speaking in soft and gentle tones of voice. The salesmen treated me politely.

I returned to Esther's house.

Esther, who had finished her housework, announced that she was going to take me to meet Dr. Shalom Srebrenik.

It was around eleven when we arrived in the Sanhedria section of Yerushalayim. We entered a large apartment house and went down the stairway to the apartment of Dr. Srebrenik, who greeted us at the door.

He was a man in his late thirties or early forties, his eyes flashing an intelligent look. He asked us to keep our voices down, as his wife was resting. It was a modest apartment, with a small kitchen and a small living room. Esther introduced us and told him about me. She followed Dr. Srebrenik into the kitchen where he prepared coffee and pancakes while listening to her. I was standing in the hall, casting curious glances into the living room. I heard him explain to Esther that I would have to attend the seminar. I did not know what this seminar was all about, and I decided that it was all a waste of time.

Entering the living room I was struck by an amazing sight: a huge bookcase full of *sifrei kodesh* (religious books) extending over the full length of the living room. These were no secular books. I stood there, entranced by the sea of books in all sizes and colors. The brilliant rays of the sun entering through the partially closed blinds reflected against the gold lettering on the backs of books, creating a dazzling aura, making it appear as if the books were glowing with a celestial shine. I was spellbound, staring at the marvelous light. It seemed as though the splendor was emanating from the *sefarim*, as though the wisdom contained in these books was illuminating the room.

I could not hear what Dr. Srebrenik was discussing with Esther, and I really did not care. The impressive library told me enough about Dr. Srebrenik. I went back into the kitchen where he served me a cup of tea, and we engaged in small talk. He was a gracious and very kind man.

I did not join the seminar that Dr. Srebrenik recommended, but over the years I heard a great deal about his lectures in which he taught Torah with wisdom and true love of the Jewish people.

By the time we came home it was already afternoon. I hurried to return to Pisgit. I had a long journey ahead of me. Uzi was waiting for me at home.

Before leaving I asked Esther to tell me how she and Yehudah had decided to choose the path of Torah.

"Yehudah, who is an engineer by profession, always had a leaning toward spiritual matters," she told me. "He dabbled in philosophy and various spiritualistic techniques for personality development. At one point, we joined a cult, and he decided to go to the United States for further study and to become a leader in the cult. A few months after we came to Seattle, Washington, *Chanukah* arrived.

"The streets and the non-Jewish homes were decorated with colorful trees and ornaments, and in the windows of the Jewish homes, the lights of the *menorah* were flickering brightly.

On the first night of *Chanukah*, ours was the only home that had no celebration. Suddenly, the bell rang. A young man with a beard, *peyot* and a black hat was standing at the door.

"'We've heard that there's a Jewish family living here,' the young man said with a shy smile, so we decided to bring you a *menorah* and some *latkes.*' He was an emissary of Chabad, the Lubavitch Chassidic movement.

"We accepted the *menorah,* thanking the young man from the bottom of the heart.

"That night we lit the *Chanukah* lights, and for the first time in our lives we felt genuinely proud to be Jewish. We began to discuss the emotion and the uplifting feeling we had experienced with the kindling of the *Chanukah* lights. We arrived at the conclusion that America and the cult had nothing to offer us. Spirituality could be found only in *Yiddishkeit,* back home in Yerushalayim.

"A short time after returning to Yerushalayim, we met Dr. Srebrenik. We attended his seminars in Arachim, and became full-fledged observers of Torah and *mitzvot.*"

En Route Home

I said good-bye, picked up the books I had bought and took the bus home. After making myself comfortable I took out the *Sefer Mesillat Yesharim* by Rabbi Moshe Chaim Luzzatto, known as the Ramchal, and I began to read.

"The underlying principle of saintliness and the basic element of perfect service of Hashem is for man to know clearly and plainly what his duty is in the world, and what he should focus on and strive for in all his labors throughout his life.

"Our Sages have taught us that man was created for the sole purpose of rejoicing in Hashem and deriving pleasure from the splendor of His Presence; for this is true joy and the greatest pleasure that can be found. The place where this pleasure may truly be enjoyed is the World to Come, which was specifically created for this purpose, but the path to attaining our desire is this world, as our Sages have said, 'This

---

world is like a vestibule to the World to Come.' (*Avot* 4:21)

"The means which lead a man to this goal are the *mitzvot* which God has commanded us. The only place where the *mitzvot* can be performed is this world.

"Therefore, man was placed in this world first, so that by these means [the *mitzvot*] which were provided for him here, he would be able to reach the place which had been prepared for him, the World to Come, where he would be satiated with the goodness which he acquired through them. As our Sages have said, 'Today you perform [the *mitzvot*] and tomorrow you receive their reward.' (*Eruvin* 22a)

"And when you look further into the matter you will see that only attachment to God constitutes true perfection, as King David said, 'But as for me, nearness to God is good,' (*Tehillim* 73:28), and 'One thing I asked of Hashem, only that do I seek: to live in the house of Hashem all the days of my life, to gaze upon the beauty of Hashem to frequent His Sanctuary.' (*Tehillim* 27:4) For only this is the true good, and anything besides this that people consider good is nothing but emptiness and misleading futility."

The lucid language of the Ramchal instantly had me spellbound. As I continued reading the book, I suddenly noticed that the person sitting across the aisle from me, a soldier in uniform, was peeking into the book with obvious interest. When I looked at him he apologized.

"Forgive me for asking you," he said, "but there's something I don't understand. The book you are reading doesn't fit the clothes you're wearing."

I was confused and did not know what to say. I simply changed the subject, answering his question with a question of my own.

"Tell me, what prompted you to look into my book?"

"You know," he replied, "I'm coming from the *Kotel* (Western Wall) right now."

"Why did you go to the *Kotel?*"

"I just completed a stint in the reserves," he replied. "My outfit suffered heavy casualties in the war in Lebanon. The men were talking about it all the time. Therefore, our company commander decided that at the end of our active duty we should all go to the *Kotel* to pray. It was not mandatory, but everyone went anyway. When I got to the *Kotel* I started crying. I don't know why, but I just cried."

"But you're not religious," I said.

"Right. I'm not religious. But I'm a Jew."

I was very moved by what he said.

I looked out the window at the late summer scenery. The parched earth was thirsting for a drop of water. The words from the *siddur* came to mind.

"Bestow your blessing upon us, God our Lord, this year, and all of its types of produce for good. And give a blessing (in the winter we substitute 'and bring dew and rain for a blessing') on the surface of the earth. And satisfy us from Your bounty . . ."

Initial Steps

Arriving home, I found Uzi sitting on the couch in the living room, reading a book. Smiling, I placed the books I had bought on the table.

"By the way," I said casually, "I've decided to observe *Shabbat*."

"You must be kidding," he answered condescendingly. "Sit down. Have a bite to eat and a cup of tea before you start making resolutions."

"No," I insisted. "I want you to know that from now on I'm going to keep *Shabbat*. To put it another way, I won't drive, light a fire or turn on the light or the television set on *Shabbat*."

He looked at me as if I had lost my mind. He had no doubt that I meant what I said, but since he was a perceptive person he decided it would be better to wait for supper time to placate me and bring me back to my senses. He went into the kitchen and warmed up something. Meanwhile, he tried to soften me up and explain to me the consequences of my bizarre plan.

I told him about the *siddur*, but this did not impress him in the least. The point that concerned him more than anything was the problem of television.

"Where am I going to watch Friday night television?" he said with a look of desperation.

"At the neighbors," I said, shrugging my shoulders.

Patiently and lovingly, Uzi tried to explain to me that I could not unilaterally impose upon him a new and different way of life, but I stubbornly refused to give in.

"If you're bored," I said, "I'll get books for you to read on *Shabbat*."

The first *Shabbat* went by peacefully. Uzi tried to cooperate in an effort to preserve the domestic peace and in the hope that my madness would blow over. On Friday night, we did not recite *Kiddush*, because we did not know how. Then we visited our neighbors, and this way we "had the privilege" of watching television. Uzi remembered that our neighbors owned a *Siddur Rinat Yisrael*. This led the conversation onto the subjects of the *siddur*, *Shabbat* and *Kiddush*.

"We learned how to recite *Kiddush* when we stayed in Canada," the neighbor told us. "Occasionally, we say *Kiddush* here, too. Why don't you come over and join us for *Kiddush* next Friday night?"

The month of *Tishrei* arrived. We fasted on *Yom Kippur*, and by studying a number of books on the subject, our commitment to *Shabbat* observance became stronger and stronger. Gradually, Uzi grew to enjoy keeping *Shabbat*.

"It's like stopping the world, getting off and climbing into another dimension," he would say.

The most difficult aspect of our new life was changing ingrained habits, adopting new ways of personal conduct and different ways of dressing, remembering not to turn the light on or off, for me to wear a skirt instead of slacks and for Uzi to wear a *yarmulka*. At first, the changeover seemed to us like a comedy, as if we were saying, "From now on, this is not me any more; I am someone else who is wearing different clothes and acting differently." Many people who want to return to the way of Torah find it difficult to deal with the negative reactions of their friends and neighbors, but we simply did not care.

I remember vividly the thrilling feeling I had each time I performed a *mitzvah* for the first time. I was moved to tears. What is so special about lighting two small candles? What is so touching about that? I realized that my emotion stemmed from something hidden deep inside me, an awareness that the *mitzvah* I was doing had an effect in the realm of the spirit and was, in essence, the fulfillment of the Divine plan.

I once read a story about a famous eccentric actor who persistently tried to join an exclusive country club, but always without success. After many years he finally got a letter of acceptance. "Never mind," he wrote back. "I don't want to join any club that is interested in the likes of me." This story depicts to a certain extent the ambivalent feelings I had. I had a strong desire to be accepted in the "King's Palace." I also sensed that I was welcome to enter the "King's Palace." But I was ashamed, thinking that it was improper for people like myself to be associated with the "Royal Palace."

King David poignantly expressed my feelings, as it is written, But I am a worm, less than human, scorned by men, despised by people. (*Tehillim* 22:7) Nevertheless, I felt it my duty to change.

I understood that if I wanted to do Hashem's will I had to live by certain laws, the same way that a person who wants to settle in any given country must abide by the laws of that country. It was difficult, because there was no one forcing me to behave like this. I was doing it by virtue of my free will; I freely chose to live according to the laws of the Torah, laws that demanded that I dress and behave modestly, that I exercise self-control in the way I express myself. It was as if a person was forced to suppress his innate "nature" and counteract impulses and desires he seeks to satisfy in his life. There was no outside force that made me do it. There was no police department to enforce these laws. It was a self-imposed discipline that I chose of my own volition. Since I wanted to become a princess in the "Royal Palace," I had to conduct myself according to the rules of "Royal Etiquette." And the Royal Book of Rules is the Torah.

The story of the beard will illustrate the situation we found ourselves in. At a certain stage, Uzi began growing a beard. We would often visit my mother-in-law, and we continued doing so after we began to observe Torah and *mitzvot*. When she noticed the first fuzz of a beard on the face of her beloved son she became very angry. For a long time she tried to convince him to shave his beard, offering a variety of strange reasons.

All the explaining we did was pointless until we reminded her that even as a young man Uzi once had grown a beard.

"Sure, but that was a different beard!" was her immediate response.

We all had a good laugh. She understood very well that this beard was a Jewish beard, a beard of self-sacrifice, whereas the earlier beard stood for protest and rebelliousness. She was upset because this was a Jewish beard.

After *Sukkot*, one of the women of Pisgit told me that Erez, one of the Pisgit residents, had become a *baal teshuvah*. Curious to find out more about it, I approached him.

"What made you decide to return to the Torah way of life?" I asked him.

"I had to be in Haifa on business, on *Sukkot*," he related. "Walking along a residential street I passed a *sukkah*. Out came a *chassid* of Lubavitch who invited me in for a *lechayim*. I went in, had some cake and whiskey, and I liked what the *chassid* was telling me very much. In fact, it inspired me to do something Jewish. I decided to put on *tefillin* every day. That's all there's to it."

My heart jumped for joy. What wonderful *hashgachah peratit*! How magnificently Hashem guides the path of every one of us individually! The fellow was on the right track, and before long we would have someone to talk to. With the help of his wife Chemdah, a warm, sensitive and very hospitable person, my hope became a reality. Within a short time, the family became complete *shomrei Torah umitzvot*.

One evening, the doorbell rang. We opened the door, and to our surprise, there was our friend Binyamin, carrying two heavy suitcases. Binyamin was the young man who had introduced us to the cult of meditation. For seven years, we had not seen him, yet there he was, a figure from a long-forgotten past. He had just arrived from New York, at Ben Gurion Airport where he took a taxi, heading straight for our house in Pisgit.

His blue eyes sparkled with joy, and he smiled from ear to ear. I thought to myself that his stay at our house would give me the opportunity to "repay" him for introducing us to meditation. We would "return the favor" by bringing him into a community of keepers of Torah and *mitzvot*.

During his sojourn at our house we had many discussions about religion and Judaism, and in the end, Binyamin returned to the United States loaded with Torah commentaries and literature on Jewish ethics and *chassidut*.

One Friday night after *Kiddush* and the *Shabbat* meal, we went for a walk on the rocky mountain. The dazzling view of the starlit sky had a soothing effect. We came upon a pile of rocks and sat down to gaze at the twinkling lights in the valley. The night was perfectly still, the mountain air pure and invigorating.

We talked about the things that occupied our minds. We felt that we lacked someone who could guide us along the new road we had chosen. We came to the conclusion that it was impossible that there would be no answers to the questions that were troubling us.

"I have a feeling that there is a person who can help us," I said to Uzi. "But I think that he lives far away."

We decided that I would go to Haifa on Sunday to discuss with the rabbi the things that were on my mind.

The rabbi received me most graciously, and I immediately began by setting forth to him all my questions. He suggested that I turn to a prominent rabbi who lived in New York, the Lubavitcher Rebbe. I knew instantly that I had found the person I was looking for. The rabbi gave me the address of the Rebbe, explaining to me that this rabbi was the leader of the Chabad movement.

That very same day I bought kosher *mezuzot* for our house, and we began observing the *mitzvah* of *mezuzah*.

I wrote a lengthy letter to the Rebbe in which I described the story of my life, beginning with my *kibbutz* years until the juncture we had reached at this moment. It took me several weeks to compose the letter, and only two months later did I manage to mail it to the Rebbe. A detailed reply from the Rebbe arrived a short while later. Let me quote a few paragraphs that are relevant to every Jew:

> In your entire long letter regarding the questions
> you have, the crises you are confronted with etc., you
> do not mention anything about performing acts of
> kindness toward other people through welfare and
> charitable institutions and the like.
>
> It is self-evident that every man and woman must do
> his utmost in this regard in order to repay in part his
> debt to society for the benefits he reaped from it by
> being brought up, educated and having his talents
> developed.
>
> I will mention you at the holy graveside.

The Rebbe's letter won our hearts for its simplicity and its
common sense approach, which can be summed up in one
phrase: We must perform acts of goodness and kindness to
others. Period.

A New Discovery

O n one of my trips to Haifa, I entered a religious book store, looking for a special kind of book, an interesting book about Torah and Jewish thought.

Scanning the books on the heavily packed shelves, one title caught my eye. The book had a strange-sounding name: *Tanya*. I lifted it from the shelf and browsed through the pages. Although printed with Hebrew letters, it used a terminology that was baffling to me. I did not recognize any of the expressions the author used. Although it was very difficult to understand, there were a few passages that did make sense to me.

The salesman was a young man wearing black clothes, a large black *yarmulka* and a beard that had barely begun to sprout. His piercing dark eyes, which were recessed in his lean and bony face, gave him an otherworldly look. I went over to him and inquired about the author whose name appeared on the title page: Rabbi Shneur Zalman of Liadi.

In a friendly and patient manner the young man explained it to me.

"The official title of this book is *Likutei Amarim*," he said. "It is popularly called *Tanya* because that is the opening word of the *sefer*. It was written by a rabbi named Shneur Zalman. "He was born in 1747 and died in 1812, and for the final decade of his life, he lived in Liadi in White Russia, hence the name Rabbi Shneur Zalman of Liadi. He is the founder of the Chabad branch of *chassidut*, also known as the Lubavitch branch of *chassidut*. Chabad *chassidim* also call him Der Alter Rebbe. The *Tanya* is indeed the fundamental text of the *Chabad* movement. The purpose of the *Tanya* is to teach one how to serve *Hakadosh Baruch Hu*."

The young man's words aroused my interest. Perhaps this book would explain to me what it is that induces *chassidim* of Lubavitch to seek out Jews and teach them about *mitzvot*? Perhaps I would find out what motivates a Jew to stand all day at the main bus station in Tel Aviv and persuade people passing through to put on *tefillin*? He certainly does not get paid for his efforts. Perhaps this book would tell me what inspires the Lubavitcher Rebbe?

I skimmed through the book and read a few random paragraphs. In Chapter Twenty-One I read: "Hashem hides Himself, withholding His endless light, in an act of Divine withdrawal, to the extent necessary in order that the world may exist, since within the actual Divine light nothing can maintain its own existence."

I was stunned. I thought that this book was talking about the light I had perceived, the light that is hidden from mankind.

I sensed that this book was something special, and I

quickly paid the salesman and left the store. I wanted to get home as fast as possible and start reading this unique book.

It took me forever to get home. The bus was delayed, and when it finally came, it moved very slowly. I did not want to read on the bus; I wanted to wait until I was home and could read in peace, alone. I wanted to try to understand it in depth.

Uzi was not at home. I sat down on the easy chair and started to read. I reread the same sentence many times, trying to understand its meaning.

Much as I tried, I could not fathom the meaning. Much later, after studying the *Tanya* with qualified teachers I gained a little superficial understanding of a few details.

In Chapter Two, I learned that the soul of a Jew has a variety of spiritual levels. To begin with, the soul gives the body its life, movement and propagation of the species, the life force that vivifies all living creatures. On this primitive level it is called *nefesh habahamit*, "the animalistic soul." On a higher level—above this elementary soul—there exists the divine soul, or *nefesh elokit*. It is a particle, a spark of Hashem Himself, so to speak it is the "spirit in man," as it is written, He breathed into his nostrils a soul of life. (*Bereshit* 2:7)

I read that when a person contemplates the greatness of Hashem he arouses within himself a sense of awe and deep respect for Hashem's infinite exaltedness. As a next step, a powerful love of Hashem is ignited in his heart, a yearning to unite with the infinite Essence of Hashem, a state that is called *kelot nefesh*, "the craving of the soul," as it is written, My soul thirsts for You, my body yearns for You. (*Tehillim* 63:2)

As I was reading this, tears welled up in my eyes. I suddenly remembered the strong feeling I had of overpowering love for the Great Light, how the Great Light was beckoning me, and I recalled the urge I sensed to nullify myself and become one with the Great Light.

In Chapter Four, I read that every *nefesh elokit,* Divine soul, is clothed with three garments—thought, speech and action—and that the study of Torah and the performance of *mitzvot* therefore clothe the soul, so to speak.

The Torah has been compared to water. (*Bava Kama* 17a) Just as water flows from a higher to a lower level so has the Torah descended from the spiritual world until it clothed itself in corporeal substances and in things of this world, such as *tzitzit, lulav, shofar* and the like. Thus, the Torah and its six hundred and thirteen *mitzvot* "clothe" the soul with all its six hundred and thirteen organs. Hence, it has been said, "Better one hour of repentance and good works in this world than the whole life of the World to Come." (*Avot* 4:17)

Hashem's Divine Presence is everywhere. But in the material world His Presence is hidden. It is manifest only when the material is nullified. I understood why we cannot perceive the Divine Light inside our body. It is because our body is not nullified; it is a tangible entity. It is "something." Hashem is manifest only when there is complete self-renunciation.

In Chapter Nineteen, I read that a soul is like a flame of a candle which by its very nature moves upward, because the fire of the flame wants to free itself from the wick and unite with its universal root of fire above.

Like the flame, the soul, too, has an innate desire to depart the body and attach itself to its Divine Root, notwithstanding that in so doing it becomes null and void and loses its identity.

In Chapter Thirty-Six, I learned that Hashem created the universe so that He may have a dwelling place in the lower worlds, especially in our world which is the lowest world of all, where darkness reigns supreme and light is shut out completely. Hashem's intention was to turn this darkness into light. This is to be accomplished by virtue of the fulfillment of *mitzvot*. To this end, Hashem gave the Torah to the Jewish people. The Torah enables us to receive the Infinite Light, the *Or En Sof,* in its pure form. Thus when we study the Torah and perform the *mitzvot*, the "darkness" of this world is turned into "light."

In the era of *Mashiach*, the revelation of Godliness will be manifest to all the nations of the world, as it is written, Reveal Yourself in the majestic grandeur of Your strength over all the dwellers of Your inhabited world. (*Mussaf* of *Rosh Hashanah*) This is the culmination of the creation of the world and the fulfillment of the purpose for which it was called into being.

Something of this revelation has already been experienced on earth at the time of the giving of the Torah, as it is written, You are the ones who have been shown, so that you will know that Hashem is the Supreme Being, and there is none beside Him. (*Devarim* 4:35) This is so because the revelation of the Ten Commandments constituted the epitome of the entire Torah, which is God's will and wisdom, without concealment of the Countenance.

Uzi had joined me in reading the *Tanya*, and we ended with Chapter Thirty-Seven, where the Baal Hatanya states that the coming of *Mashiach* depends on the *mitzvot* we fulfill during the *galut* (exile). By performing a *mitzvah* one draws down Divine Light into the physical world. If you just show a willingness to do Hashem's will He will enable you to attain the greatest heights.

We read in *Shir Hashirim* 5:2, I was asleep, but my heart was wakeful. Hark, my beloved knocks! Let me in, my sister, my love, my faultless dove!

Who is the beloved? It is *Hakadosh Baruch Hu* Whose voice

is calling the people of Yisrael, "Let Me in, My sister!" She is the beloved who is a captive of the long dark *galut. Hakadosh Baruch Hu* asks Yisrael, "Allow Me to come in. You take the first step; you take the initiative. If you make an opening as small as the eye of a needle, I will make an opening for you as wide as the gate of the Hall of the Sanctuary." If we but make a small beginning, Hashem will respond by showering on us all the blessings of His good treasury. With each *mitzvah* we perform we bring the redemption a little closer.

Although I could not understand the full meaning of these profound concepts, I did understand that by performing the *mitzvot* we attain a greater attachment to Hashem. As a reward for the performance of each *mitzvah* Hashem reveals more of His great light. Each *mitzvah* draws more Divine light from the higher spheres to the physical world, until at the time of the *geulah sheleimah*, the ultimate redemption, the whole world will be filled with knowledge of Hashem, as it is written, For the earth shall be filled with knowledge of Hashem. (*Yeshayahu* 11:9)

Having read the *Tanya*, the puzzling behavior of the Lubavitcher *chassidim* became clear to me. Now I understood why they are always on the go. They feel that there is not a moment to lose, that every minute in which they don't do Hashem's will is wasted time. Every Jew who does not carry out Hashem's *mitzvot* is a loss to the Jewish people.

Encounter in Yerushalayim

A year later, a few weeks before *Chanukah,*
my friend Esther called, suggesting that I
come to Yerushalayim to attend a lecture by Rabbi
Schwartz. I decided to go. She had invited Rabbi Schwartz to
deliver a private lecture in her house, but she did not tell me
the topic he was going to discuss.

I took the bus to Yerushalayim. In the seats in front of me
two young men were sitting, one wearing a beard and obviously religious, the other not religious. They struck up a
conversation, and as they were talking, the religious young
man tried to explain to the other that every human being has
a soul and a specific task to fulfill in the world.

"When a person dies," he argued convincingly, "his soul
goes up to a higher world, the *Olam Ha'elyon.*"

"That can't be true," the other fellow replied with a
mixture of surprise and indignation. "Those stories about the
hereafter and higher worlds, they're all fairy tales. Only one

thing is sure; nobody has ever come back from there!"

I felt like interrupting and telling him that his friend was right, that the *Olam Ha'elyon* does exist, that I had been there and come back. But I thought it would be wiser to keep quiet and not to say anything. I knew that it would not do any good, and he would not believe me anyway. He probably would say that I had lost my mind. I kept to myself.

By the time I arrived at Esther's house the furniture had already been moved out of the living room and replaced by neat rows of folding chairs.

Toward evening the apartment began to fill with people, and finally Rabbi Schwartz arrived, looking pale but cheerful. He had a distinguished look, black hair and a black beard with a touch of grey. He was wearing a black suit and a black hat. Even his shoes were black. His burning, penetrating eyes made you feel as though he could see right through you. After taking his seat in the armchair provided for him he launched into his lecture without any introductions or digressions.

The room was absolutely quiet. When Rabbi Schwartz spoke, no one even dared whisper. Not a sound was heard. His discourse was a torrent of inspiring thoughts, a stream of profound insights. As he spoke, his piercing eyes swept across the faces of the audience.

He enlivened his address with exciting and humorous anecdotes and by realistically acting out situations or mimicking personalities. The audience listened with utter fascination. I felt that his heart was in it and that he deeply cared about each and every single Jew. He was saying the things he felt he had to say.

The gist of his message was clear and to the point: If we want the *geulah sheleimah*, the final redemption to arrive, we must do *teshuvah*. There is no time to waste.

At the end of his speech I went over to him.

"I have a story to tell that might interest you," I said. "I'd like to relate to you a very unusual experience I lived through, but I simply don't have the courage to talk about it with so many people milling about."

He gave me an appointment to come and see him the next day at his office in the *yeshivah* he had founded, *Yeshivat Kehillat Yaakov.*

The following morning, I travelled to the *yeshivah*. It was a bright, clear Yerushalayim morning. There is something about the Yerushalayim air you don't find any other place in the world; it has a purity and bracing freshness that is un-equalled. The deep blue sky of Yerushalayim lifts the spirit like no other sky in the world.

I waited outside, enjoying the invigorating atmosphere, until Rabbi Schwartz finished *Shacharit* and invited me to come in. His office was small and furnished very sparsely. I was impressed by the simplicity of the decor and the pleasant reception I was accorded. Rabbi Schwartz listened in silence as I recounted my story, his serious face betraying no emotion. He did not seem surprised; my story held nothing new to him.

"I'd like to publicize your story," he said.

"I promise you, I'm going to put my entire experience into writing," I replied.

In the course of our conversation he drew the inference that Uzi was not yet putting on *tefillin*.

"Abba! Father!" the rabbi called out at once.

There appeared in the door a dignified gentleman with a long white beard whose calm demeanor reflected a deep inner serenity. The man was Rabbi Schwartz's father. The old father placed before me on the table a beautiful pair of *tefillin*, a *tallit* and a velvet gold embroidered bag.

"The *tefillin* are for Uzi. If and when you have the money you can pay for them."

Rabbi Schwartz's eyes were flashing with excitement. He began to pull several books from his bookcase, moving with the agility of an athlete while speaking to me earnestly and with great emphasis.

"There are five basic *mitzvot* a Jew is required to observe: *Shabbat, tefillin, taharat hamishpachah, kashrut* and *mezuzah.*"

Four of these we were fulfilling already. Now the *tefillin* were lying in front of me. It was an offer that could not be refused.

"What can you tell me about your family?" the rabbi asked.

"My parents are very simple hard-working people," I answered. "As a matter of fact, they live in a *kibbutz*. There is really nothing special about my family."

"Isn't there a rabbi somewhere in your background?" he persisted.

Suddenly, I remembered the story my grandmother told me many years ago.

"When I was a young girl," I replied, "my grandmother had told me that her father was a rabbi and a *kabbalist*, a descendant from a prominent Sefardi family that originated

---

* Editor's note: Following is a list of the names of the illustrious *ge'onim* of the Alfandari dynasty and the works they wrote. The Alfandari family traces its lineage to the tribe of Yehudah, specifically to Betzalel, the divinely inspired master artist and builder of the *Mishkan*.

Rabbi Chaim Alfandari I, 1588-1640, served as rabbi in Constantinople, studied under the famous Rabbi Yosef di Trani. His responsa are printed in *Maggid Mereshit*. He wrote *Derech Hakodesh* on the sanctity of Eretz Yisrael.

Rabbi Chaim Alfandari II, died in 1733, son of Rabbi Yitzchak Rafael Alfandari, and grandson of R. Chaim Alfandari I, studied under his father and his uncle, R. Yaakov Alfandari. He served in the rabbinate of Conin Spain. His name was Rabbi Alfandari."*

When I mentioned my great-grandfather's name, Rabbi Schwartz reacted with deep agitation.

"There's the answer!" he exclaimed in an emotion-filled voice. "Now it all becomes perfectly clear. The reason you were allowed to return was not because *you* begged for it. Your plea to return to life was answered in the merit of your ancestor who was a *tzaddik* and a *kadosh* (a holy man). I presume that he approached the *Kisei Hakavod*, the Divine Throne of Glory, to implore Hashem and appeal to Him that you be given another chance. You have no idea what great and saintly rabbis your ancestors were. They belonged to a family of towering Torah giants. Countless people, among them great rabbis, came to receive blessings from your saintly

---

stantinople. In 1713, he travelled to Eretz Yisrael where he stayed for four years. The Chida in his *Shem Hagedolim* calls him "the marvel of our generation" and praises his "eloquence, erudition and his many awe-inspiring deeds." Rabbi Chaim II wrote *Esh Dat*, sermons and responsa.

Rabbi Yaakov Alfandari, uncle and mentor of Rabbi Chaim II, wrote *Mutzal Me'esh*.

Rabbi Eliyahu Alfandari, died in 1717, He served as Rabbi of Constantinople, studied under R. Moshe Benveniste, author of *Pnei Moshe*. Rabbi Eliyahu wrote *Michtav Me'eliyahu*, on *gittin*, and *Seder Eliyahu Rabbah Vezuta*, on the subject of *agunot*.

Rabbi Aharon Alfandari, died in 1774, serving as Rabbi of Smyrna. In his later years he moved to Eretz Yisrael and died in Chevron. The Chida writes in his *Shem Hagedolim* that he knew him personally and "enjoyed the radiance of the light of his Torah and his holiness." The Chida reports that he personally heard Rabbi Aharon tell him that he (R. Aharon) descended from the tribe of Yehudah and was of the direct lineage of Betzalel. Rabbi Aharon Alfandari wrote Yad Aharon, a commentary on the *Tur*, and *Mirkevet Hamishneh*.

Rabbi Yosef Alfandari wrote *Vayikra Yosef*, responsa and sermons, and *Yavo Halevi*, novellae and Torah commentaries, and *Porat Yosef*, responsa.

Rabbi Shlomo Elazar Alfandari wrote *Knei Avraham*, responsa, and *Maharsha*, a *halachic* commentary.

---

ancestors. Do you think that anyone who asks to be returned to life has his wish fulfilled, just like that? Let me assure you, yours is a very unusual case."

The moving words of Rabbi Schwartz affected me deeply. I was upset over the fact that I, a descendant of *tzaddikim* and *kedoshim,* did not know what a *siddur* was until I was thirty years old. This lack of knowledge was the result of my being taught that the world has no Ruler or Creator, that everything happens by "chance," that everything came into being "by itself," that man does not owe a reckoning to anyone.

I was a *tinok shenishbah,* a "child that was taken captive, and raised by kidnappers who did not reveal to him his true identity or heritage." My parents, too, fell into this category. They also had been estranged from their legacy. I sensed that this was to be my test and my task in life, to establish anew the dynasty of my glorious ancestors.

Rabbi Schwartz made me aware that nothing in the world was more important for me than to attempt to follow the right path, the path of the Torah.

When I said good-bye, he invited Uzi and myself to spend a *Shabbat* with him.

As promised, I wrote my story and mailed it to him.

A Jewish Shabbat

*J*t was now a few weeks later. The idea of having to spend a *Shabbat* with Rabbi Schwartz did not appeal to Uzi. He tried everything to get out of it. On the appointed Friday morning he said that he was not sure we would be able to go. "Let's wait until this afternoon."

The hours went by. Would we or wouldn't we go? I was nervous, but I was determined not to get into an argument about it. In the afternoon, Uzi announced, "Okay, let's go."

It was only four hours until *Shabbat*, and the ride to Yerushalayim would take three and a half hours at best. We started out. I prayed that we would arrive in time for *Shabbat*.

We drove down from Pisgit via the Bet Hakerem Valley, then after making a right turn, headed south along the Jordan Valley. Uzi was edgy, and his anxiety made me tense. He stepped on the accelerator, trying to gain time. I was not sure whether we would get to Yerushalayim before the onset of *Shabbat*. It seemed as though he had done it on purpose. I did not understand what was bothering him. Why couldn't we have left in the morning? I said nothing, not a word. It was *Erev Shabbat*, and we were going to light the eighth *Chanukah* light, the beginning of the charming winter season in Eretz Yisrael.

I looked out over the greening fields sprouting a blanket of tender light green growth. We passed olive groves and groves of saplings that were beginning to show their first buds. The scene reminded me of Rabbi Schwartz's speech about this magnificent world. How *Hakadosh Baruch Hu* prepares the fruits for us, makes them ripen on the tree in order that we may have food to eat. How utterly marvelous! All we have to do is plant a seed, and Hashem issues the command, "Grow!" Then He causes the fruit to ripen and paints it in a variety of enchanting colors. All this he does to keep us alive. What incredible wisdom and infinite creativity we are witnessing each and every day! How can we remain indifferent and close our eyes to this flow of plenty that is bestowed on us? How can we be ungrateful and not thankfully acknowledge Hashem's goodness by saying a *berachah* over the fruit?

The sun descended toward the west as we began our climb toward Yerushalayim. In the distance the settlement Maaleh Adumim came into view. About twelve more miles to Yerushalayim the lush green of the Jordan Valley changed into the stark barrenness of the arid desert. The road wound its way along rows of rugged, craggy hills. Time was running out. Uzi was driving at top speed, racing the setting sun. The sun almost touched the treetops, time for *hadlakat hanerot*, candle lighting time was almost here.

We entered Yerushalayim from the east, driving through the first streets which were in an Arab neighborhood. The road wound its way up a hill coming to an intersection at the summit. Suddenly, Uzi slammed his foot on the brake; our car came to a screeching halt, giving us both a sharp jolt. From the opposite direction, coming straight at us, a Volkswagen van carrying fifteen Arab passengers was trying to stop, and with a grinding, grating, rattling sound crashed into our car. Oh, no! An accident! The front of our car was smashed. And here it is *Erev Shabbat*, just a few minutes until candle lighting time!

The passengers on the Volkswagen began to scream. I did not understand what the screaming was all about, but afterwards they explained to us in English that a child aboard the van had been injured. They took her straight to the hospital. Our main concern was not to be stuck here on *Shabbat*. Uzi exchanged information and licenses with the driver of the Volkswagen. We tried to think of a way out of our predicament.

"Should we take a taxi? But how can we abandon our car here in the middle of the highway?"

"Let's try to get the car moving," Uzi said.

He turned the key—the engine started. We drove our car with its smashed front end. I felt that this obstacle was a test, as if an unseen hand was trying to keep us back.

We were a strange sight. Now it really was beginning to get dark. A few minutes after the sounding of the first siren announcing the imminent arrival of *Shabbat* we entered the Kiryat Sanz section of Yerushalayim. People dressed in their Shabbat finery were walking to *shul* calmly and sedately. Some of the youngsters, suspecting us of wanting to desecrate the *Shabbat*, angrily shouted at us, "*Shabbos! Shabbos!*"

We are also *shomrei Shabbat*! I thought to myself. We're on your side! If only you knew!

When we arrived at Rabbi Schwartz's home everyone breathed a sigh of relief. We immediately lit the *Chanukah* lights and the *Shabbat* candles. It was truly a miracle that we made it in time to be able to experience the four highlights that coincided: *Shabbat, Chanukah, Parshat Miketz* (the portion of the week *Miketz*) and the home of the Schwartz family. It was a small and modest apartment consisting of two small bedrooms, a narrow kitchen and a small dining room. In the Schwartz family there were eight children, *ken yirbu,* and a great deal of *simchah.* It was a family that served Hashem with genuine gladness. There was a smile on everyone's face and a kind word on everyone's lips, bringing joy to others. Everyone was contented, far more content than the rich people living in mansions of the exclusive Savyon neighborhood of Tel Aviv. The faces of the parents and the children radiated happiness.

In the dining room, a large table was set, covered with a sparkling white tablecloth, a bouquet of fragrant roses in the center. The tranquility was almost palpable, especially after the frenzied day we had gone through.

This was the first time that I had the privilege of experiencing a hallowed family atmosphere like this, the spirit of pure *kedushah.* The lights were burning, the sun had set. Looking out the window I was greeted by a spectacular view. All the windows of the large apartment houses around us were illuminated with the glow of *Chanukah* lights. Thousands of small flames flickering. Then came *Kiddush* followed by the *Shabbat* meal. I tasted the uplifting joy of the spirit of *Shabbat,* the *zemirot* and various *niggunim.* The smiling faces of our hosts mirrored their *nachat,* the pleasure they had from their offspring. The gracefully served meal was interspersed with interesting Torah thoughts and animated Torah discussions in which everyone participated. True, the apartment was small, but there was room for all. Evidently, the members of this family took up less space for themselves. The main thing was, the home was permeated with joy and faith.

The sound of harmonious singing filled the room, the hauntingly beautiful melody eloquently expressing the words of *Tehillim*. The melodies were enchanting. With rising fervor the men sang the *niggunim*, their eyes closed in concentration. I was overcome with the spirit of *Shabbat*. This is a family with endless love for their fellow Jews, I thought. They give and give without a grain of selfishness. I regretted that I did not grow up in an atmosphere like this, in a milieu filled with pure *bitachon* and *simchah*.

The *Shabbat* meal ended. The smaller children who had begun to play returned to their seats, and together the family recited *Birkat Hamazon* in a quiet tune. Then everyone went his separate way, and Uzi and I remained at the table with the rabbi, who delighted us with Torah thoughts which he illustrated with fascinating tales about rabbis.

"Let me tell you a story I heard from Rabbi Tzvi Enbel," the rabbi began. "A scientist wanted to convince his atheist colleague that the universe was created by God. What did he do? He built a miniature planetarium in his house, showing the sun, the earth, the moon and the planets whirring in their orbits. Admiring the planetarium, his non-believing colleague asked, 'Who made this?'

"'This came into being all by itself,' his friend replied.

"'Are you joking?' replied the atheist. 'A mechanism like this doesn't just happen!'"

"If a planetarium can't create itself, then the universe itself with its myriad stars and heavenly bodies most certainly did not arise by accident. The Creator in His wisdom brought it into being.

"There is only one absolute truth. The God of truth will not give His Torah to His nation in a way that is open to doubt. Any religion that originates with one man who claims that the truth was revealed to him is implausible and highly suspect. If a man states that he is sent by God, and that God told him to change the Torah, what proof does he offer to back up his claim?

"All religions begin with one man, except Judaism. Judaism originated in the presence of six hundred thousand people—people who are skeptical by nature—who saw and heard Hashem's revelation on Mount Sinai. You can fool some of the people some of the time, but you can't fool all of the people for hundreds of generations until this day.

"Our tradition which was handed down from father to son began when six hundred thousand people witnessed Hashem's glory. Hashem says, 'You have seen that I spoke to you from heaven.' (*Shemos* 20:19)

"Until one hundred and fifty years ago secularist Jews did not exist. Jewish teaching was passed on from generation to generation for 3300 years. A normal father will not lie to his son about fundamental principles. Millions of parents will not lie to millions of children throughout the course of Jewish history. If our ancestors had not actually witnessed the *Kabbalat Hatorah*, the Receiving of the Torah, they would not have told it to their children."

The rabbi spoke with deep fervor. I sensed how much the alienation and the estrangement of so many Jews in our generation was hurting him.

On *Motzei Shabbat*, Rabbi Schwartz arranged a *Chanukah* gathering for hundreds of people in a large hall in Yerushalayim. At this occasion he wanted to read to the audience the story of my life which I had written to him. My husband and I were bewildered. Rabbi Schwartz asked us to attend the assembly. We had no way to get out of it, but we made up our minds to disappear the moment people would try to identify us. It was a bizarre feeling to have an experience that was so deeply personal and so uplifting to me publicized, and to think that people might not believe it. It was an experience that had become part of our daily lives, and yet, there might be those who would dispute its authenticity. We had to dig up every ounce of courage we had to be able to enter the hall.

Rabbi Schwartz read my letter to the entire assemblage, and everyone listened intently. When he ended, the hall was thrown into commotion. We quickly slipped outside and left with a sense of great relief. I had done all I was required to do to let the world know about the miracle I had experienced. I was hoping that others would draw the proper conclusions from it.

Meeting the Rebbe

*T*he years passed, and we continued to live the Torah way of life. Meanwhile, we were blessed with an addition to our family by the birth of our daughter Channah, or Channie, as we call her affectionately.

As time went by, we gradually grew closer to the Lubavitcher Rebbe. We wanted very much to see and get to know the Rebbe "who kindles the lanterns," the souls of the Jewish people. We felt a need to try to understand the secret of his charisma. Why, from the very beginning, did I sense such strong trust and affinity to this Rebbe? Why had he taken the trouble to associate with us, and why was he interested in helping us?

We decided to fly to New York to visit the Lubavitcher Rebbe. But then I thought, Isn't it rather odd to travel such a great distance just to go and see a rabbi?

First, there was the problem of lodging. Where would we stay for three weeks? Staying at a hotel would cost more than we could afford. I called an acquaintance in Kfar Chabad and told him our problem.

"No problem," he replied. "I'm going to give you the telephone number of the Josephy family who lives near the Rebbe's residence. You'll be able to stay with them."

This is interesting, I thought. Who would put up a family of total strangers for a three weeks' stay?

I was in a quandary: to call or not to call? In the end I got the nerve and placed the call. To my delight, the voice on the other end was that of a lady who spoke Hebrew like a native-born Israeli.

"My name is Sarah," she said in a congenial tone, "and I'm inviting you to come and stay with us. For how long would you like to stay?"

"For about two weeks," I answered; I did not dare say "three." Besides, I thought, let's get there first, and then we'll see.

"Are you sure it's okay?" I asked.

"Yes, perfectly all right. Don't worry about anything."

"Thank you very much," I said as I put down the receiver. Imagine, a woman who did not know us was willing to take us into her home!

Two weeks later, Channie and I set out on our journey on a non-stop flight to New York. Uzi would join us after a short stay in Europe where he had to be on business.

The plane, which departed in the middle of the night, roared off into the dark, rapidly gaining altitude.

"We have reached an altitude of thirty-four thousand feet, so I'm turning off the seatbelt sign," the resonant voice of the captain came over the public address system.

I recalled an anecdote about a *chassidic rebbe* who was flying in a plane to New York. When the captain made the announcement about the altitude at which the plane was flying the rebbe said, "Very strange, the captain is telling us that we have reached a height of thirty thousand feet, but I don't see anyone in this plane being lifted to a higher level, not even by one inch."

After a twelve hour flight, we landed at Kennedy Airport at six o'clock in the morning. At last, the wheels of the plane touched the runway. It was still dark outside, but coming in for the landing, we could see the bright lights of New York City. As the huge jet was moving slowly toward the gate, dawn began to break over the eastern sky.

Passport check, baggage pick-up and customs formalities were finally over. Outside a blustering, frigid wind greeted us. It almost blew us away. As the sun rose over the horizon, we were chilled to the bone. I pushed the baggage cart, dragging Channie behind me.

"Taxi!"

"Where to, lady?"

"770 Eastern Parkway. Crown Heights, Brooklyn." It was the address of Chabad headquarters.

In the hall of the Rebbe's house, scores of people were patiently waiting for the Rebbe to arrive. I found out that this scene repeated itself several times a day at "770." As the hour of the Rebbe's arrival approached, the crowd of people grew larger. The youngsters were standing near the entrance to the Rebbe's office, waiting to receive a coin for *tzedakah* from the Rebbe. I entered the small waiting room and positioned myself behind the young boys. Suddenly, excited whispers could be heard.

"*Der Rebbe geht!* The Rebbe is coming!"

Twenty or thirty people squeezed into the area in front of the Rebbe's study. The crush seemed almost unbearable, but the men did not seem to mind.

The Rebbe made his entrance and with a quick look surveyed the entire assemblage. His look was much more than a cursory glance. With his eyes he established contact with one and all. I felt as though he were telling me personally, "Yes, I know that you are here."

The Rebbe's features reflected wisdom. His blue eyes bespoke purity and kindness. I felt warm tears streaming down my cheeks as a yearning for Torah welled up in me.

The crowd eagerly pushed forward toward the Rebbe; but surprisingly, around the Rebbe there was no crowding. Everyone respectfully kept his distance as the Rebbe began to distribute *tzedakah*—coins to the children. The Rebbe held each child by his right hand, looked into his eyes as he placed a coin into his hand. One after another, the children received the coins, thus they were taught an unforgettable lesson in the *mitzvah* of *tzedakah*. Then the Rebbe strode to the *tzedakah* boxes and dropped a few coins into each box. After concluding the giving of *tzedakah*, the Rebbe entered his private study. The surge of exhilaration abated.

The people began to stream out of the building. It was hard to believe that a crowd this size could fit into the small area of the hall. Channie stayed next to the the Rebbe the whole time. Now she came over to me, clutching the Rebbe's coin tightly in her little fist.

"Mommy," she said with child-like innocence, "when the Rebbe put the coin into my hand there were tears in his eyes!"

She looked wan and pale, but her eyes glistened with excitement.

The people dispersed in all directions. Going out into the street I suddenly felt lightheaded, as though walking in a dream-world. In one hand, I was carrying a suitcase, in the other a handbag. Channie held on tightly to my blouse. In her other hand she clutched the Rebbe's coin. We were going to the Josephy residence on Kingston Avenue.

Our ringing woke Mrs. Josephy. She answered the door, and upon entering, I noticed the disarray that told me that other guests had left only hours earlier. They had departed just as we arrived. Sarah welcomed us with a friendly smile and offered us a cup of coffee. At long last, we could rest up from the wearisome trip.

A Farbrengen

*T*hat evening, a *farbrengen* was scheduled to take place at "770." At a *farbrengen*, the Rebbe delivers a scholarly lecture that is interspersed with joyous singing and the handing out of small cups of vodka to the assembled for a heartfelt *lechayim* wish by the Rebbe. A *farbrengen* is not a routine affair; it is held in honor of a special occasion or an anniversary of an important date.

This particular *farbrengen* was being held in honor of the 19th of *Kislev*, the day on which Rabbi Shneur Zalman of Liadi (the Baal Hatanya) was released from prison one hundred and ninety years ago. As early as seven o'clock in the evening the huge *beit hamidrash* (hall for prayer and study) began to fill up. Thousands of people converged until there was standing room only. At nine-thirty, a hush fell over the hall. The Rebbe entered. A path was cleared for him through the sea of people to enable him to reach his seat at the large table on the platform in the center of the hall. Seeing the Rebbe march to his seat was a spectacle reminiscent of the parting of the Red Sea.

A rousing song burst forth from the throats of thousands of *chassidim*. The Rebbe was seated, and gesturing with his hands, he encouraged the men to continue singing.

The Rebbe cast his eyes over the entire assembly. Everyone could feel that the Rebbe was relating to him individually, arousing the deep recesses of his soul with that penetrating look.

With a slight motion of his hand the Rebbe brought the singing to a halt. Absolute silence dominated the scene. The *farbrengen* was about to begin.

The Rebbe spoke in Yiddish. The audience listened with rapt attention to his words of profound wisdom and insight.

After about forty-five minutes, the Rebbe interrupted his discourse. Everyone joined in an inspiring song and poured a small cup of vodka. The Rebbe drank *lechayim* with all his *chassidim*. Once more his eyes swept across the hall. Like radar, he captured the gaze of everyone individually and sent him his *berachah*. Somehow, an inner connection with the Rebbe was established by virtue of this eye contact. This spiritual bonding was an amazing phenomenon. After ten or fifteen minutes of wishing *lechayim*, the Rebbe continued his address for another forty-five minutes with similar interruptions of song and well-wishing. The entire *farbrengen* lasted several hours.

Since I was not taught Yiddish in the *kibbutz* I was forced to put on the headpiece and listen to the simultaneous translation. I wondered why the Rebbe spoke in Yiddish. I would have liked to ask the Rebbe personally, but I was just one among an audience of several thousand people. How could I possibly get through to the Rebbe? But I was wrong. I evidently did get through to him somehow. During this *farbrengen* the Rebbe mentioned my name several times while explaining chapter 90 in *Tehillim*. The first verse of this psalm reads, *"Hashem maon hayita lanu*, Hashem you have been our *maon*, our refuge, in every generation." The last verse of the psalm reads, *"Vihi no'am Hashem Elokeinu aleinu*, May the *noam*, the favor, of God our Lord be upon us." The letters of the word *maon* are the same as those of *noam*, which happens to be my last name.

The Rebbe explained that this psalm refers to man's life on earth, as *maon* alludes to *Olam Hazeh* (This World), for it is man's task to make the world a refuge and dwelling place for Hashem. When his task is completed he merits *noam*, favor, which is a reference to *Olam Haba*, the World-to-Come.

Two days later, at the *farbrengen* of *Shabbat*, I received the full answer to my question. The Rebbe must have "heard" my question, since he spent several minutes explaining why he speaks in Yiddish. I could not understand what he was saying because on *Shabbat* there is no simultaneous translation. But on Sunday, reading the Hebrew translation of his speech, I could not believe my eyes! The Rebbe explained that the Baal Shem Tov used to say his Torah insights in a language other than *leshon hakodesh*, the holy tongue. This practice was followed by his successor, the Maggid-Rabbi Dov Ber of Mezritch, the Baal Hatanya and all the *rebbes* of Lubavitch and other branches of *chassidut* who delivered their Torah thoughts specifically in Yiddish and not in Hebrew. The reason for this was that in those days most of the Jews in Eastern Europe spoke Yiddish. When an insight is expressed in the vernacular it is better understood and penetrates the hearts of the listeners.

The Rebbe also added that, although Yiddish is not the same as *leshon hakodesh*, over the generations this language has nevertheless attained a degree of *kedushah* of its own by virtue of the fact that for close to a millennium the Jewish people studied Torah and expressed the highest concepts and conversed in this language.

I was moved to the core of my soul. Not even a mother can detect the innermost thoughts of her only child the way the Rebbe had "heard" the vibrations of my heart.

The story is told that on one occasion, a group of scientists engaged the Rebbe in a discussion. One of their questions was, "What is the task a Rebbe must fulfill?" The Rebbe answered as follows: The prophet describes the Jewish people in terms of "for you shall be the most desired of lands." (*Malachi* 3:12) A Jew is likened to land, to earth. The earth holds many treasures, minerals, precious metals and jewels. But you must know where to find them and how to extract them from the earth. If you don't know where to look for gems, all you will dig up will be mud, stones and rocks. The same is true for the human soul. Some psychiatrists analyze the human soul and discover nothing but mud and dirt, others find rocks and stones. The rebbe's task is to uncover the genuine diamond that is hidden in every Jew, his divine soul.

On Sunday, the Rabbi has the custom of handing out dollar bills for *tzedakah*. Thousands of people line up in front of his house, waiting patiently for long hours. The Rebbe gives a friendly greeting and a *berachah* to everyone and hands him a dollar bill. Through this warmhearted encounter everyone develops a strong personal attachment to the Rebbe. The distribution of dollar bills lasts for many hours during which time the Rebbe hands out thousands of dollars, which the recipient, in turn, gives to a worthy cause.

Channie and I were standing in a line which extended all along the street. There were separate lines for men and women. Alternately, the ladies' and men's line would move forward as it passed in front of the Rebbe. It was quite cold, about thirty-two degrees Fahrenheit, but I felt warm inside. A police patrol was stationed in front of the building to keep order, but there was no need for it. Several young men quietly and effectively supervised the progress of the advancing lines.

Before I knew it, I found myself standing in front of the Rebbe. He looked at me and gave me a dollar bill. His bright blue eyes were shining, and his radiant face had a glow of kindness. I will never forget his gracious look, a fatherly look that penetrated to the depth of my soul.

"*Berachah vehatzlachah!*" he blessed me. "Blessings and good fortune!"

"Please, Rebbe, give me another *berachah.*"

"*Besuros tovos!*" the Rebbe wished me, as the lady behind gently nudged me forward. "Glad tidings!"

Sightseeing in New York

*A*fter the ritual of receiving the dollar bill, Channie and I boarded the subway to go sightseeing. The cashier gave us a map of the New York subways.

Channie was overjoyed: "A train that rides underground. How about that!"

The train arrived at the station jampacked with people. I decided to go to Central Park in the heart of Manhattan. We sat down in the one vacant seat we were able to find. I studied the map and, naively, planned to get off at the station on the north side of the park in a neighborhood called Harlem. Next to me a young black man was sitting, with large eyes and an intelligent expression. Channie looked at him with amazement; she had never seen a black person before in her life.

The young man smiled and began to talk to me.

"I can tell that you don't live here," he said. "Where are you from?"

"We are from Israel," I replied.

"Wow!" he said. "And where are you heading for?"

"We're going to Central Park, and this is where we want to get off," I said, pointing out the Harlem station on the map.

His expression became very grave.

"Oh no, you'd better not," he warned. "Don't you get off here! You folks get off at 96th Street. Don't go into Harlem. It's dangerous!"

I thanked him for warning us.

"Why did you come to New York?" he asked.

"We came to see the Rabbi of Lubavitch."

"I see," he said as he got up. "I've heard many things about this rabbi. He is a very famous man around here. Well, good luck. I'm getting off at this station."

When we got off the train, a gray-haired black woman came in our direction. Passing us, she noticed Channie laughing and jumping.

"No wonder she's laughing," the elderly woman mumbled, as she went her way. "She has her whole life ahead of her."

We visited the zoo in Central Park. Channie enjoyed playing in the playground and watching the squirrels scampering about. After spending a delightful afternoon in Manhattan, we returned to the Josephy home.

One morning, Miriam, a friend of the Josephy family, took us to Prospect Park to take her children and Channie ice skating. Miriam used to live in a *kibbutz* but left Eretz Yisrael to study medicine and settled in America. While the children were enjoying themselves on the ice, we went for a nice walk in the big park. We talked about the institution of marriage. I told her about the Jewish approach to marriage, about the union of two souls, about the harmony that exists in a Torah-oriented marriage. Miriam, who was listening attentively, came to a sudden halt and looked at me with her blue eyes.

"I wonder why they never told us about any of these ideas in the *kibbutz*," she exclaimed with surprise.

"I've been asking myself the same question," I replied.

"I'm convinced," Miriam continued, "that if I had known these things in the past I wouldn't have gone through so many crises and hardships in my life."

I agreed with her. "Apparently, this was a test we had to pass," I said. "We are the products of the community that raised us this way, and now it is our duty to break with the past and recognize our true identity. I don't think it pays to become depressed about things that happened in the past. Hashem, Who is compassionate and beneficent gave us this test. We have the obligation to be upright, and then His light will shine on us."

Every morning, Channie and I went to see the Rebbe, and she was fortunate enough to get another coin from him. We bought a little purse—she picked a pink one—in which she put her coins. The entrance hall was so crowded with people that I preferred to remain outside. I placed Channie among the children and waited. Standing amidst the children were mothers holding their babies in their arms. The babies, too, were given coins. The mothers, visibly moved by the experience, left with their babies through a back door.

"Why are you crying?" I asked one of the mothers.

"I don't know why," she replied. "When I'm in the presence of the Rebbe I'm simply moved to tears."

It was the first night of *Chanukah*. The entire neighborhood was filled with cars and *"mitzvah* tanks," vans with large *menorot* strapped to their roofs. The Rebbe kindled the first light on a very large golden *menorah*. The *beit hamidrash* was buzzing with the voices of thousands of people. The outside temperature was below freezing, yet inside the air-conditioning was in operation, and in spite of this, it was very warm. The voices of thousands of *chassidim* resounded in a full-throated rendition of *Hanerot Halalu*. The Rebbe was standing erect, immersed in deep thought.

The vast multitude, the Rebbe, the *Chanukah* lights, to me it all was an overwhelming event. In my mind's eye, the flickering flames represented thousands of yearning Jewish souls. When the singing ended, the Rebbe began his discourse. At the conclusion, the Rebbe, aided by young men, distributed dollar bills to the thousands of people in the huge throng.

Slowly the crowd began to disperse. The cars displaying *menorot* on their roofs wound their way to Manhattan in a long brightly lit procession, for a parade along Fifth Avenue. I imagined the tens of thousands of people who would be watching the parade in amazement.

The entire city was bathed in light. In the large apartment houses, the lights of thousands of *menorot* shimmered in the windows. In the large parks and prominent public squares, gigantic *menorot* had been erected which were lit every night. Not far from the *menorah*, decorated pine trees could be seen— two opposites standing side by side.

We heard that in the evening a *menorah* would be kindled in one of the large squares of Brighton Beach, a neighborhood where many Russian Jews have settled. A few of the girls planned to attend the ceremony, and I decided to join them. Coming down the stairs of the subway station, we were greeted by the sound of *chassidic* music. Channie jumped for joy. Nearby, a huge *menorah* had been installed, and next to it a *chassid* was playing a keyboard. Small *menorot* had been placed on a platform, along with candles and brochures explaining the meaning of *Chanukah* in Russian and English. Their curiosity aroused, a few people began to gather around the platform.

The young *chassidim* started the celebration with a lively dance, dragging the shy spectators into the circle with them. Gradually, the circle of dancers widened as more and more people joined enthusiastically, their faces radiating true happiness. The celebration lasted for an hour and a half, as a growing number of people took part in the festivities.

The following day, Uzi arrived. He told me that, just as he arrived at "770" from Kennedy Airport by taxi, the Rebbe was leaving his office and greeted him with a wave of his hand. He was thrilled that his first welcome in America was the Rebbe's friendly smile.

We waited impatiently for *Shabbat* to arrive. On *Shabbat* there would be another *farbrengen*. On Friday night, the Rebbe kindled the *menorah*, and after *davening*, we went to the Josephy family for the *Shabbat* meal. Sarah had prepared a lavish feast, explaining that she was expecting additional guests. As it turned out, she had about ten guests for the Friday night *seudah*. The *seudah*, which lasted several hours, was enlivened with *zemirot* and insights on the weekly Torah portion.

On *Shabbat* morning, when I wanted to go to the *beit hamidrash*, Channie insisted that I stay home. After a long debate, she finally agreed to come along with me to *daven*. By the time we arrived, the *davening* was almost over. I found a seat in a corner of the ladies' section and started to *daven*. When the congregation ended *davening*, I was still in the middle of my *Shemoneh Esrei*.

The Rebbe remained in his place, and everyone was waiting. A few minutes later, the Rebbe turned around and strode toward the exit. I followed him with my eyes, but I stayed in the *beit midrash* with Channie, to wait for the *farbrengen* which was scheduled to start at one-thirty in the afternoon. Many men and women likewise remained in the *beit midrash*.

In the interim, ladies brought in pots full of steaming hot *cholent*, cake and grape juice for *Kiddush*, which they offered to the people who stayed in the *beit midrash*. We were very grateful for their warm hospitality.

At one-thirty, the Rebbe returned, and the *farbrengen* began. The hall once again filled up rapidly. The speech was again in Yiddish; I could not understand one word. After about two hours, Channie managed to drag me outside, and we went back to the Josephy home.

Mrs. Josephy greeted us with a warm smile and a puzzled look in her eyes. "Why did you leave before the end of the *farbrengen?*" she asked.

"Channie became very restless, and besides, I did not understand one single solitary word because the Rebbe spoke in Yiddish."

"True, you didn't understand, but your soul listened and understood."

Sarah's words brought back the memory of the accident, of my soul leaving my body. I understood what she meant, and I knew that she was right. The soul can indeed hear. We talked about the soul and the body and the connection between the two, about life and death and about the future revival of the dead.

Sarah listened to my comments with great interest and added her own comments. We really understood each other, and I was fortunate to count her as my friend.

Inexorably, the day of our return trip came ever closer. We said good-bye to the Rebbe at the "dollar bill ceremony" on Sunday. The Rebbe gave us an additional dollar bill to give to a charitable cause in Eretz Yisrael, thereby appointing us as his emissaries for fulfilling the *mitzvah* of *tzedakah*. I wanted to tell the Rebbe that I would like to welcome him in Eretz Yisrael with the coming of *Mashiach*, speedily in our days, and that I really did not want to say farewell, but I was pushed forward. I am sure the Rebbe "heard" my thoughts, as I was being moved along in the line.

We thanked the Josephy family for their gracious hospitality and drove off to the airport. I was happy to return home, to my beloved country, the land about which the Torah says, the eyes of God your Lord are on it at all times. (*Devarim* 11:12)

Homeward bound on the plane my thoughts returned to the Rebbe, the *beit midrash* and to various incidents and experiences. Channie asked me for her pink purse. She wanted to play with the coins the Rebbe had given her.

Emptying the purse, she said, "Mommy, they're not shiny anymore!"

"What do you mean?"

"The shiny coins. When the Rebbe put the coins into my hand they were shiny. And now the shine is gone!" She was disappointed.

Everything seemed like a dream. It was the same feeling I had during the accident when my entire life passed before my eyes like a mirage.

A Closing Word

During recent years, since we commenced observing Torah and *mitzvot*, I began to feel true joy and the meaning of *simchah* of *kedushah*, joy that is inherent in holiness and purity. It is pleasure that is enjoyed by body and soul alike and grounded in the belief that *Hakadosh Baruch Hu* guides the world. For much of my life, I did not know the joy of *Shabbat*, *tefilah* or *taharat hamishpachah*. Now I am free of worries. I feel that there is Someone Who cares for us, Who nourishes and sustains us, Who fills all our needs.

I have the freedom to enjoy and celebrate the holy *Shabbat* with lighting candles, a sparkling white tablecloth, wine and *challot*, and to listen in tranquility to the *Shabbat* hymns. I have the freedom to fulfill *mitzvot* that elevate body and soul into a state of exalted *simchah* that I never knew before.

I have this marvelous sense of knowing that we are building a dwelling place for Hashem, for the beloved Creator

Who bestows infinite happiness on us.

A building crew that puts up an ordinary structure has a sense of satisfaction when the building is completed. From the architect down to the manual laborer, the more impressive the building, the greater their happiness. How much deeper is the inner satisfaction when the crew is erecting a dwelling place for *Hakadosh Baruch Hu,* the infinitely great King of kings. All of us are on that building crew, so shouldn't we do our utmost to do our work to perfection?

Anticipating the *geulah* is no longer an abstract concept for me. I vividly remember the scenes I witnessed and the feelings that moved me. I am sure that the *geulah* will come very soon and that presently we are living in the days of *atchalta degeulah,* the advent of the *geulah,* the final days of the *galut.*

I believe that I was allowed to return to my body in order to have a last chance to achieve *tikkun,* to correct my own soul and to do my share in putting the world in order. Our generation is perhaps the first one in which so many out-of-body experiences have been reported. In earlier times, this was virtually unheard of. Now, while we are in *galut,* corporeal bodies in a material world, we have the opportunity to cling to Hashem by doing *mitzvot* and studying the Torah and gather up the holy sparks, the estranged Jewish souls trapped in the captivity of the *galut.*

Our life on earth may be compared to the parable of a king whose life was saved by a simple peasant. "As a reward for your good deed," said the king to the peasant, "I will permit you to enter my treasure-house which is filled with treasures from all over the world. For one hour you may gather up anything your heart desires, and it will be yours to keep."

In order to make this hour more enjoyable for the peasant, the king arranged to have enchanting music piped into the treasure-house. Enthralled with the beautiful music, the simple peasant sat down and dreamily listened to the bewitching melody. When the hour was over, the king's chamberlain asked the peasant to leave. To his dismay, the peasant realized that he had wasted his chance of acquiring the huge fortune that would have allowed him to live in comfort for the rest of his life.

Man, like the peasant in the parable, wastes his allotted time in This World, enthralled as he is by its temptations and alluring siren song. When his time is up, and his soul has to depart the world, he is distressed to realize that he has neglected to garner the rich fortune of *mitzvot* and *maasim tovim* that were his for the taking.

The human soul, the spiritual element in man, is a fragment of the Divine light, of the absolute Truth, of Hashem; it is the *chelek Elokah mimaal*.

The answer to every question of life is bound up with the recognition that it is Hashem Who sustains all of existence, that He bestows on us His flow of abundance both in a material and a spiritual sense.

It is my fervent wish that the *Ribbono Shel Olam*, Who revealed Himself to us on Mount Sinai and Who has manifested Himself in the Torah, may shower on us His infinite light of exalted goodness at the *geulah sheleimah*, the final redemption, speedily in our days. Amen.

Glossary

alav hashalom: rest in peace
baruch Hashem: Blessed is the Name; thank Heaven
be'ezrat Hashem: with G-d's help
berachah: blessing
chalutzim: pioneers
Chazal: Sages
Gemara: Talmud
geulah: redemption
Hagomel: thanksgiving prayer
Hakadosh Baruch Hu: the Holy Blessed One
Hashem: G-d
hashgachah pratis: providence
ir ketanah: small town
kedushah: holiness
kehillah: community
kesher: bond
levayah: funeral
maasim tovim: good deeds
Mashiach: the Messiah
midat harachamim: divine mercy

Mishkan: Tabernacle
mitzvot: commandments
nes: miracle
neshamah: soul
olam: world
olam hazeh: this world
Rosh Hashanah: Day of Judgment
Shabbat: Sabbath
Shechinah: Divine Presence
sheker: falsehood
shivah: mourning period
simchah: joy
tallit: prayer shawl
Tanach: Bible
tefillin: phylacteries
Tehillim: Psalms
teshuvah: repentance
treif: unkosher
yetzer hatov: good inclination
yetzer hara: evil inclination
yishuv: settlement
Yom Kippur: Day of Atonement